PENGUIN MOD

Mottled Dawn

SAADAT HASAN MANTO, the most widely read and the most controversial short-story writer in Urdu, was born on 11 May 1912 at Samrala in Punjab's Ludhiana district. In a literary, journalistic, radio scripting and film-writing career spread over more than two decades, he produced twenty-two collections of short stories, one novel, five collections of radio plays, three collections of essays, two collections of personal sketches and many scripts for films. He was tried for obscenity half a dozen times, thrice before and thrice after Independence. Some of Manto's greatest work was produced in the last seven years of his life, a time of great financial and emotional hardship for him. He died several months short of his forty-third birthday, in January 1955, in Lahore.

KHALID HASAN, journalist, writer and translator, was born in Srinagar, Kashmir. He has translated most of Saadat Hasan Manto's work. He has also translated the stories of Ghulam Abbas and the poetry of Faiz Ahmed Faiz. Khalid Hasan's own publications include *Scorecard*, *Give Us Back Our Onions*, *The Umpire Strikes Back*, *Private View* and *Rearview Mirror*. He lived in Washington and was the US correspondent for *Daily Times* and the *Friday Times*, Lahore. Khalid Hasan passed away in February 2009.

DANIYAL MUEENUDDIN's debut collection of short stories, *In Other Rooms, Other Wonders*, was the winner of the Story Prize, the Rosenthal Family Foundation Award from the American Academy of Arts and Letters, and the 2010 Commonwealth Writers' Prize (Best First Book, Europe and South Asia). It was also a finalist for the National Book Award, the Pulitzer Prize, and for a number of other awards. The book has been published in twenty-three countries.

Mueenuddin spent his childhood in Lahore, where Manto wrote so many of the stories in this volume, and grew up hearing Manto's name. He now lives in South Punjab.

SAADAT HASAN MANTO

Mottled Dawn

FIFTY SKETCHES AND STORIES OF PARTITION

Translated from the Urdu by Khalid Hasan
With an Introduction by Daniyal Mueenuddin

PENGUIN BOOKS

PENGUIN BOOKS

USA | Canada | UK | Ireland | Australia
New Zealand | India | South Africa | China

Penguin Books is part of the Penguin Random House group of companies
whose addresses can be found at global.penguinrandomhouse.com

Published by Penguin Random House India Pvt. Ltd
7th Floor, Infinity Tower C, DLF Cyber City,
Gurgaon 122 002, Haryana, India

First published in English by Penguin Books India 1997
First published in Penguin Modern Classics 2011

10 9 8 7 6 5 4 3 2

ISBN 9780143418313

Typeset in Sabon by R. Ajith Kumar, New Delhi

Printed at Repro Knowledgecast Limited, India

www.penguin.co.in

This mottled dawn
This night-bitten morning
No, this is not the morning
We had set out in search of

—Faiz Ahmed Faiz

In memory of Saadat Hasan Manto
and
his dream of a subcontinent where people will live as people, irrespective of religion, caste or colour, where hatred shall stand abolished, where hypocrisy shall have no sway, where religion shall only ennoble those who follow it, not divide them into warring tribes.

Manto's dream remains a dream.

CONTENTS

A TWIST WITH DESTINY

Daniyal Mueenuddin

Nehru's 'tryst with destiny', his pretty phrase describing Independence—which as a child I understood as a 'twist with destiny', twist as in the waltz, the Watusi, the twist—was more a rape than a tryst or a twist, one of the great catastrophes of the twentieth century. My father, who was Rehabilitation Commissioner in Lahore at the time of Partition, had the gruesome task of meeting the trains that came into Lahore from Indian Punjab, freighted with a load of corpses, butchered en route by Hindu and Sikh mobs—just as some functionary on the opposite side had the task of meeting at Delhi's station death trains loaded with slaughtered Hindus and Sikhs. My father found no difficulty in explaining the mass killings, saying that, if today it were announced that all red-haired men could be killed with impunity, tomorrow there would not be a red-haired man alive. Such is human nature. It is this quality in mankind that Saadat Hasan Manto, his horror moderated by his grim humour, bears witness to in the volume of stories that you hold in your hands.

Some sixty years after Partition, we inevitably still read these stories as historical documents, recording those events. There are still people living who remember the bloodshed, who suffered personally from the violence. We, in both India and Pakistan, are still crippled by the narratives that the armies of our countries have built around the crimes of Partition, cynically keeping the hatred generated at Partition alive, in order to justify their budgets and their dominant roles in their respective countries. The Pakistani military, from the moment of my country's inception, has sat on and smothered the country's political body, justifying itself by reference to the Indian threat. The Indian military, bloated upon a larger corpus, operating more discreetly, has played a similar game. We may yet all be blown to kingdom come in revenge for the killings of 1947.

If we today keep our grievances alive, so many years later, it is startling that Manto, writing soon after these events, was able to be so level-headed, so cool. That he was able to withhold blame. Although the stories in this book are specifically about a political event, about the dilemmas of people caught up in a great internecine massacre, they are neither overtly nor covertly partisan. They espouse no position and are almost purely descriptive. As Chekhov has famously said, the writer's task is not to pass sentence, but rather, to empathize with his characters' sufferings after they have been judged and condemned. In these stories, Muslims, Hindus and Sikhs are all guilty of murder, of inhumanity. The catastrophe is general. Manto's dominant attitude, in the face of this madness, is one of bemusement at the absurdity of the violence. Men and women, who have lived together in peace, when given licence to kill do so with relish, with abandonment.

The key to Manto's attitude lies perhaps in the story 'A Tale of 1947', which is based on a reminiscence he wrote soon after Partition. A Muslim character named Mumtaz, closely identified with Manto himself, is taking a ship from Bombay for Karachi. The narrator, one of three Hindus sending Mumtaz off with a final carouse, considers why he has decided to leave them.

> Mumtaz was very emotional that day. The three of us had come to see him off. He was sailing for Pakistan, a country we knew nothing about. All three of us were Hindus. We had relatives in West Punjab, now Pakistan, some of whom had lost their lives in anti-Hindu riots. Was this why Mumtaz was leaving us?
>
> One day Jugal had received a letter which said that his

> uncle who lived in Lahore had been killed. He just couldn't believe it. He had said to Mumtaz, 'If Hindu-Muslim killings start here, I don't know what I'll do.'
>
> 'What'll you do?' Mumtaz had asked.
>
> 'I don't know. Maybe I'll kill you,' he had replied darkly.
>
> Mumtaz kept quiet and for the next eight days he didn't speak to anyone; on the ninth day he had said he was sailing for Karachi that afternoon.

While it might appear that Mumtaz is leaving from fear of being killed, the story instead conveys with characteristic lightness, without emphasis, that, in fact, Mumtaz is leaving because he bows to the inevitability of its being so: that there must be blood, that their difference as communities has divided them. This is pique, not pressure. This is sublime: he obeys the historical imperative. There is no anger in him, but rather the tenderness that a man feels upon leaving a woman whom he has loved deeply, upon abjuring a great love. Pointing to the horizon, where sea and sky are joined, he says, 'It is only an illusion because they can't really meet, but isn't it beautiful, this union which isn't really there?' Mumtaz's response to the separation imposed by Partition is aesthetic rather than political.

This response is also romantic, and perhaps naive—without blame there can be no justice—and yet, is a key to our understanding of why Manto's stories of Partition are so very good. As in Isaac Babel's *Red Cavalry* stories, which describe the savagery of the Russian revolution, the horror of such events is best conveyed through the lens of a romantic sensibility. Manto was, by all accounts, a gentle, wounded, disorganized man, and therefore well suited to consider in his stories these massacres, his softness marrying their violence. One of my elderly relations, ancient in my childhood, bless her, and now gone to the reward that she so fervently believed in, happened in the 1950s to live in the same building where Manto came to rest: Lakshmi Mansions on the Mall road in Lahore. She recalled him well, a drunken pathetic figure, scribbling away for the newspapers; an artist, which in her eyes made him little better than a tramp. And yet, in these stories, Manto triumphs over the unlit urinous stairwells of Lakshmi Mansions, over the petty disapproval of his neighbours, over his poverty, his brutal hangovers; he even triumphs over the fact of Partition. When the last mourner has passed away, after the last child who lost his parents is dead, these stories will be read, unmoored from the suffering that they memorialize.

This individual triumph correlates to the triumph that we, his readers, experience, over the particular infamies of Partition, and the general violence and randomness and brutality of life. Through these stories we are enabled to make sense of the violence depicted: to make sense of it not rationally but emotionally. If Manto's intention was not political, was not to identify with any of the factions in the disaster of Partition, the effect of his stories is certainly political, in the sense that all description is political. What the poet W.H. Auden said of Sigmund Freud might equally be said of Manto:

> He wasn't clever at all: he merely told
> the unhappy Present to recite the Past
> like a poetry lesson till sooner
> or later it faltered at the line where
>
> long ago the accusations had begun,
> and suddenly knew by whom it had been judged,
> how rich life had been and how silly,
> and was life-forgiven and more humble . . .

Manto makes us care about all the victims, and about the killers as well as the killed—it is only by caring, by empathizing with them, that we can learn to overcome our prejudices and to sublimate our desire for revenge. Reading these stories with an open heart, we are enabled to transcend our political biases—which is perhaps the most radical stage of political development.

I have been speaking of Manto's romantic sensibility, which I believe made him exceptionally suited to telling these horrific stories. It is this sentimentality, which might cloy if the subject were different, that allows us to look directly at these horrific scenes without flinching. I would also like to touch briefly on his technique, which seems equally well suited to this material. The overwhelming impression the stories leave is one of artlessness, effortlessness—which, as most writers will acknowledge, is an exceedingly difficult effect to achieve. There is, in these stories, a concentration of techniques, which are all directed to the same purposes: he aims for immediacy, vividness, concentration. He approaches his subject obliquely, writing about lunatics in an asylum, about a dog caught in no man's land between the Indian and Pakistani armies, about a public urinal—so that these stories seem to be snatched almost randomly from the whole spectacle, significant insignificant moments. There is little description of landscape, no lingering upon smells or sights, and there is almost no reflection, no editorializing upon the events he describes. Although he often uses the first person narrator, the 'I', there is almost no interiority, no rumination or description of feelings. With rare exceptions, the stories are extremely short, covering a few pages and a brief span of time.

The most striking of Manto's techniques for achieving the impression of artlessness and immediacy is found in his endings, which, in the best of the stories, manage simultaneously to be almost weightless, mere throwaways—and yet devastating. There is no great crescendo; often the stories seem not to end at all, but to trail away. Again, this is appropriate to the material. Confronted with these horrific scenes, the only possible reaction is a shake of the head, an acknowledgement of the horror. Consider the almost laconic ending of 'The Return'—I won't spoil it—or the ambiguity of the last sentence in 'A Tale of 1947'. In the hands of a lesser writer, these qualities in the stories might make them appear inconsequential.

What is consequence? And to whom? Manto draws our attention to the, literally, millions of little tragedies that together composed the whole tragedy of Partition. I spoke of my father, who at Partition met the trains coming in from India, new India, violent India, enemy India, with no one alive but the trainman, to show us on the Pakistani side that violence would meet violence, that they would kill us as we killed them. My good father walking through the trains, registering the dead—I can imagine him, with his stout walking shoes. He had from childhood hunted, for deer and partridge and wild boar—he once shot a bluebuck from the back of a horse with a pistol—and killed perhaps hundreds of crocodiles on the Indus. After he walked through these bloody trains, he never hunted again.

One day, inspecting a train come in from East Punjab, all the passengers seemingly dead, he found—or some sweeper hired to shove the bodies off the bogie found—a baby girl wedged under the mass, alive. My father took her home, and my sisters asked to keep her. Bambi—they named her Bambi—had skin pale as an Irish girl in Galloway, and bright red hair. She was brought up as one of the family—one of the family, yet not one of the family—and was given two squares, fifty acres, of land, enough to distinguish her. My father, in the following terrible months, found two other girls under the piles of bodies in other trains—I suppose the assassins for a moment felt pity, could not bear to kill those infant girls. These other two were brought home, but were not taken into the family. Instead they were sent into the servants' quarters at my father's house, and became maids.

Who was this red-haired girl? How did she come by her pale skin? And how must it have been, for the two foundlings who were not brought into the house, who were raised as servants?

This is Manto's Partition.

9 July 2011
Springs, New York

TRANSLATOR'S NOTE

The Partition of India in 1947 was a cataclysmic event. Was it inevitable? What would have been the shape of things if there had been no division? What would have been the state of relations between Hindus and Muslims? Would they have learnt to live together in amity? Or would there have been a continual civil war? While most Indians hold the Muslims responsible for the 'vivisection' of 'Mother India', the Muslims, and certainly those who became Pakistanis or came to live in Pakistan, believe that a short-sighted Congress leadership failed to furnish the Muslim minority with the guarantees and reassurances it was looking for. This could only have led to a parting of the ways.

It is argued—and evidence supporting this view continues to come to light—that had the Muslims been accorded credible guarantees of the constitutional protection of their rights and freedoms in a united India, separation may not have been their chosen option. The vast majority of Muslims who supported the demand for a country of their own was afraid that the British Raj may make way for Hindu Raj. Leadership on both sides may have erred and it is, of course, easier to be wise after the event, but it is fifty years since the British left India in the disarray in which they had found it, and the debate as to the rights and wrongs of the 1947 dispensation continues. However, it is now being increasingly felt in both countries that the time has come for the people of the subcontinent to lay aside the baggage of history and move forward as friends and neighbours into the 21st century. No enmity need last as long as this one has lasted.

The great tragedy of the Partition of India lay in the sectarian and religious bloodletting that preceded and followed it. To this day, it is not known with any degree of accuracy how many people on both sides of the divide were massacred in cold blood. Savagery such as that witnessed at the time of Partition has few parallels in history. A fierce madness seems to have taken hold of people who had lived together for centuries and, barring occasional and limited violence, in a spirit of mutual tolerance and understanding. In 1947, something snapped. The holocaust of Partition was in a way more horrifying than the extermination of European Jews by the Nazis. It was the Third Reich that undertook the liquidation of the Jewish population as a matter of state policy. The machinery of the state was pressed into service to accomplish this grisly task. It was organized and meticulously planned killing.

In the subcontinent, it was not the state that killed people but the people themselves who became the perpetrators of a vast and macabre drama of death. Overnight, civilized citizens turned into demented killers. Neighbours killed neighbours and friends killed friends. Reprisals were widespread. If a hundred men were reported killed by one community, the other community made sure that it doubled the score. There were no holds barred. Women became the worst victims of Partition. Hundreds upon thousands of them were raped, killed or abducted. No one was spared, not even children and old people. Whole neighbourhoods, entire villages were set on fire and the fleeing, screaming inmates chased and done to death with improvised weapons. No one has been able to make sense of that madness. It is clear that not only individuals but entire communities can go insane.

However, there was one man who tried to make sense of what had happened. He was not a politician—for whom he generally felt contempt—but a writer. His name was Saadat Hasan Manto. Much was written about the communal killings of 1947 but little of it has survived as literature because it was either of no higher a literary value than that of weepy, maudlin tear-jerkers or it was partisan or jingoistic. Manto alone had the detachment and the humanity to take stock of this tremendous and disturbing eruption of primaeval evil, try to comprehend it in all its dimensions and put it in perspective. It is a measure of his greatness that he did not allow the savagery of 1947 to diminish his faith in the essential rightness of human nature. He demonstrated through one powerful story after another that the intrinsic nobility of man, his basic decency, his ability to love and care may become temporarily eclipsed but they do not die. Manto's humanism, his rejection of religious labels and his refusal to accept cruelty and intolerance distinguish him from his contemporaries.

Manto left Bombay, a city that he loved and a city that he yearned for until his dying day, soon after Partition. He felt deeply disturbed by the intolerance and distrust that he found sprouting like poison weed everywhere, even in the religious world of cinema. He could not accept the fact that suddenly some people saw him not as Saadat Hasan but as a Muslim. When he learnt that Ashok Kumar, with whom he worked at Bombay Talkies, had been receiving hate-mail accusing him of being responsible for the induction of Muslims into the company, he was disillusioned. He stopped going to work and would just lie all day on a sofa in his flat staring into space. He said later that he lived in a kind of limbo. He could not think. One day it finally happened. He decided to leave Bombay and go to Pakistan, a country he did not know though he had known it when it was not Pakistan. It was a tremendous wrench which he never got over. Bombay was his first love and his fascination for the city that 'asked no questions' always stayed with him. In his final dark and drunken days in Lahore when he was dying, he used to wonder why he had done what he had done. Would Bombay remain the way it was before Partition? Would it have changed? Had it already changed? These questions kept nagging Manto as he found life getting the better of him. He never stopped wondering.

Manto wrote about his last days in Bombay in a powerful memoir devoted to his life-long friend, the debonair screen actor Shyam, who died in a tragic accident while shooting a movie a couple of years before Manto's own death.

It seems such a long time ago. The Muslims and Hindus were engaged in a bloody fratricidal war with thousands dying every day on both sides. One day, Shyam and I were visiting a newly-arrived Sikh refugee family from Rawalpindi (Shyam's hometown which was now in Pakistan) and listening in shocked silence to their horrifying story of escape. I could see that Shyam was deeply moved. I could well understand what he was going through. When we left, I said to him, 'I am a Muslim. Don't you want to kill me?'

'Not now,' he replied gravely, 'but when I was listening to them, and they were talking about the atrocities committed by the Muslims, I could have killed you.'

His answer shocked me greatly. Perhaps I too could have killed him at the time. When I thought about it later, I suddenly understood the psychological background of India's communal bloodbath. Shyam had said that he could have killed me 'then' but not 'now'. Therein lay the key to the communal holocaust of Partition.

In Bombay, religious tension was rising every day. Ever since Ashok Kumar and Wacha had taken over Bombay Talkies, most senior positions had coincidentally gone to Muslims. However, this had caused much resentment among the Hindu staff of the company. Wacha had begun receiving a steady stream of hate-mail containing threats of arson and murder, not that either he or Ashok gave a damn about that sort of thing. I reacted differently. Being sensitive by temperament, I felt greatly troubled by the prevailing atmosphere. Once or twice I expressed my sense of unease to Ashok and Wacha and even suggested that they should sack me since some Hindu employees were convinced that the Muslim influx in Bombay Talkies was entirely my doing. They said I was out of my mind.

That I certainly was. My wife and children were in Pakistan, but they had gone there when it was still a part of the India that I was familiar with. I was equally familiar with the occasional riots which broke out between Hindus and Muslims. The piece of land that I had once known as India had been given a new name. Had this changed anything? I did not know. What self-government was going to be like, I had no idea, my efforts to understand the new reality had failed to produce an answer.

Independence day, 14 August 1947, was celebrated in Bombay with tremendous fanfare. Pakistan and India had been declared two independent countries. There was great public joy, but murder and arson continued unabated. Along with cries of *India zindabad*, one also heard *Pakistan zindabad* slogans. The green Islamic flag fluttered next to the tricolour of the Indian National Congress. Pandit Jawaharlal Nehru and Quaid-i-Azam Mohammad Ali Jinnah's names were shouted endlessly by people on the streets.

I could not decide which of the two countries was now my homeland—India or Pakistan. Who was responsible for the blood which was being so mercilessly shed every day? Where were they going to inter the bones which had been stripped off the flesh of religion by vultures and other birds of prey? Now that we were free, had subjection ceased to exist? Who would be our slaves? When we were colonial subjects, we could dream of freedom, but now that we were free, what would we dream of? Were we even free? Thousands of Hindus and Muslims were dying all around us. Why were they dying?

All these questions had different answers: the Indian answer, the Pakistani answer, the British answer. Every question had an answer, but when you tried to look for the truth, these answers were of no help. Some people said if you were looking for the truth, you would have to go back to the smouldering ruins of the 1857 Mutiny. Others disagreed. No, they said, the answer lay in the history of the East India Company. Then there were those who insisted on going further back. They wanted you to study and analyse the Mughal empire. Everybody wanted to drag you back into the past, while killers and terrorists went about their gruesome business unchallenged, in the process writing a story of blood and fire which has had no parallel in history.

With one or two exceptions, all the stories that this volume contains were written after Independence in Lahore. It is ironic that Manto's most creative period should also have been his harshest in economic and emotional terms: the fact was that there was no work for him in Pakistan. The film industry in Lahore, which could have provided him with reasonable earnings, had been all but destroyed by the trauma of Partition. What studios there were had belonged to the Hindus who had left. Some films were being made, it was true, but the facilities were primitive and the funding poor. What work there was had to be shared by a large number of writers who were in even more dire straits than Manto.

Manto, living with his wife and three small daughters in a flat off Lahore's Beadon and Hall Roads, found himself struggling for a living. The only way he could make some money was by writing and that was what he did day and night. He wrote with great speed and he wrote every day. He was one of those writers who never revise anything they have written. Manto's manuscripts are a marvel—from start to finish, the hand remains steady and unusually beautiful. The first page is as neat and legible as the last. Manto was always a drinking man, but in Bombay he lived an organized life. Drinking was something he did with his close friends in the evening. In Lahore, his life came unstuck. A man of great personal discipline, he suddenly found himself without an office or place of work. In the morning, he would get ready but there was no place to go to, which led to his reckless drinking. His routine broke down and his life became unstructured. He began to drink during the day and in his last days would walk into a publisher or editor's office, ask for some paper and something to place under it and in an hour or so produce a perfect story or sketch in return for a fee that varied between fifteen and thirty rupees. Then he would go out and buy himself liquor, often the lethal, local variety.

Given this background, is it not amazing that it was during this period that he produced his most powerful work. Had he written nothing but a story like the 'Toba Tek Singh', he would have ensured for himself a place of his own in literature. Is it not a tribute to Manto's genius that despite the tyranny of circumstance, he managed to produce some of the greatest stories of all time in any language or literature.

The fifty pieces that constitute this anthology fall in two categories. First there are the stories, followed by, what for want of another word, one can only call sketches or vignettes, that make up a slim volume called *Siyah Hashye*, published soon after the division of the country. The title of the book means 'black fringe', which was how Manto saw the massive human upheaval involving millions of refugees from both sides that preceded and followed Independence. If Independence, Manto seemed to say, was something bright and good, then it was fringed with black. After the book was published, Manto was subjected to harsh personal attacks and accused of bad taste, cynicism and even cruelty. He wrote about it in 1951 in a preface to another book.

> For a long time, I refused to accept the consequences of the revolution that followed the Partition of the country. I still feel the same way; but I suppose, in the end, I came to accept this nightmarish reality without self-pity or despair. In the process, I tried to retrieve from this man-made sea of blood, pearls of a rare hue, by writing about the single-minded dedication with which men killed men, about the remorse felt by some of them, about the tears shed by murderers who could not understand why they still had some human feelings left. All this and more, I put in the book *Siyah Hashye*. I am only human, with all that being human entails. I have the same strengths and frailties which other human beings have. And, believe me, it caused me great pain when some of my literary friends made cruel fun of my book, denouncing me as an irresponsible hack, a jokester, a nuisance, a cynic and a reactionary. One of them, a close friend, accused me of having robbed the dead of their possessions to build a personal collection . . .
>
> I was angry because nobody was willing to listen to me. I was depressed by the greed and avarice with which people were enriching themselves through allotments of

> abandoned, non-Muslim properties after the Partition of the country. Everyone was jockeying for positions of profit and influence. It did not seem to occur to anyone that after such a revolution, things would never be what they once were. Nobody had the time to think. There were so many questions which went begging for an answer. Would the old values survive or would they perish? What would be the difference between a government of foreigners and a government of our own? What would the atmosphere be like? Would it be possible for ideas to flourish under the new dispensation? What would be the relationship between the individual and the state, between other entities and their official counterparts? These were grave matters that needed serious thought. No longer could we rely on foreign or imported formulas. Unfortunately, our intellectuals proved incapable of either comprehending the dimensions of the challenge or responding to it creatively. They were obsessed with themselves, their own egos, their own self-important roles . . .
>
> I may be a pornographer, a sensation monger, a cynic, a jokester and a reactionary, but I am also husband to my wife and father to three little girls. If any of them falls ill and I have to run from door to door to get her medical attention, I feel great pain and embarrassment. Yes, I have friends, but they are even poorer than I. When they are in need and I am unable to help them, I feel awful. I cannot stand human suffering, I swear to God.

In *Siyah Hashye*, except in one instance, none of the participants in the bloody drama of Partition is identified by religion, because, to Manto, what mattered was not what religion people were, what rituals they followed or which gods they worshipped, but where they stood as human beings. If a man killed, it did not matter whether he killed in the name of his gods or for the glory of his country or his way of life. To Manto, he was a killer. In Manto's book, nothing could justify inhumanity, cruelty or the taking of life. In the holocaust of 1947, he found no heroes except those whose humanity occasionally and at the most unexpected times caught up with them as they pillaged, raped and killed those who had done them no personal harm and whom they did not even know. Manto saw the vast tragedy of 1947 with detachment, but not indifference because he cared deeply.

The sketches, some of them no longer than a line or two, bring out the enormity of the tragedy set in motion by the great divide. They are deeply ironic and often deeply moving. A Kashmiri labourer finds himself in the middle of a street riot and as the crowd breaks into stores and begins to loot the goods, he too picks up a sack of rice but is chased by the police and shot in the leg. He falls to the ground and is made to carry the bag he had stolen to the police station. After he fails to persuade the police to let him keep it, he stutters, 'All right, exalted sir, you keep the rice, all poor me ask is my wages for carrying the bag, just four annas.'

In another sketch, rioters attack a home and are about to ransack it when a mysterious man appears on the scene and advises them to be a little more methodical, otherwise they would break precious objects which could be theirs whole and intact. He conducts the organized ransacking of the home till it is nearly stripped of all its valuables. And who is this mysterious man? The owner himself.

A couple save their lives by hiding in the basement of their house, but emerge a few days later to get some food and are caught by the new occupants, who happen to be members of a faith that forbids the killing of any living things. They refuse to let the couple step out and instead, send for help from a neighbouring village whose inhabitants have no compunctions about taking life. The fugitives perish eventually but the religious obligations of the pacifists are duly fulfilled.

In another sketch, a man who had stolen two sacks of sugar falls into a well while trying to get rid of them and dies. The following morning, the residents of the locality find that the water of the well now tastes sweet. The thief is immediately canonized.

Then there is the man who is accosted on a train and asked to reveal his religion. He says it is the same as that of his interrogators and swears that he is telling the truth. They are not satisfied and remove his trousers to examine if he has been circumcised, which he turns out to be. 'This is the only mistake, the rest is in order,' he pleads with them. The 'mistake' is eliminated along with its maker.

Rioters chase a man down the street, catch up with him and are about to kill him when he begs them to spare him because he is on his way home for vacation.

Two men buy a girl because she is said to be from the other religion, but after they have had their use of her are mortified to discover that they have been 'cheated' as she belongs to the same religion as they do. 'I want our money refunded,' one of them declares.

A train is brought to a stop by rioters who belong to a certain religion. Methodically, they pick out everyone who belongs to the other religion and slaughter them. Following the completion of this religious duty, they treat the rest of the passengers to milk, custard pies and fresh fruit while apologizing for the frugality of the repast on account of the short notice they had.

A man pleads for the life of his daughter. His request is granted and she is stripped of her clothes and thrown in with 'the other girls'. A train is stopped in search of 'turkeys'. Finally, one is discovered and is about to be killed in the carriage when one of the killers screams, 'No, no, not here! It'll mess up the carriage. Take him out.' A man sitting in an upstairs room takes aim at a child through a window. His companion is horrified but is reassured that though the gun is without any bullets, 'How does a little child know?'

One man who has slaughtered fifty pigs in a mosque is disgusted that he has not been able to sell any of the pork, whereas in the neighbouring country, people are queuing outside every temple to buy beef.

The greatest of Manto's 1947 stories is 'Toba Tek Singh'. This is how it goes. The madness that has gripped the subcontinent permeates even the lunatic asylums and the great decision-makers of the two countries decide that since there has been such a transfer of populations as well as assets, it is only logical that non-Muslim lunatics should be repatriated to India and Muslim lunatics in India transferred to Pakistan. On the day of the great exchange, there is only one man, Bishan Singh, who refuses to leave because he wants to stay where he was born and where his family lived, the town of Toba Tek Singh in Pakistani Punjab. The exchange takes place at the common border of the two countries. They try to push him across the line into India, but he does not move because he wants to live neither in India nor in Pakistan, but in Toba Tek Singh. They let him stay standing in no-man's-land because they tell each other that he is only a harmless old man. As the morning breaks, Bishan Singh screams just once, falls and dies. This is how Manto ends this classic parable of Partition. 'There, behind barbed wire, on the other side, lay Pakistan. In between, on a bit of earth, which had no name, lay Toba Tek Singh.'

In 'The Return', a young girl who has been recovered from India and brought to Lahore by Muslim volunteers lies on a bed in a hospital. She is comatose and has been raped so brutally by men from both sides that, when the doctor brings her distraught father in to see if she is the abducted daughter he has been looking for, she undoes the string that holds her *shalwar* in place as she hears the words 'Open it'. She pulls the garment down and opens her thighs. It was only the window in the room that the doctor wanted opened. Her father does not notice but screams with joy, 'She is alive. My daughter is alive!'

'Colder than Ice'—a story for which Manto was tried in Pakistan on an obscenity charge is about Isher Singh, a Sikh who abducts a Muslim girl during the riots and rapes her, only to realize later that she had been dead all the time. His jealous mistress, Kalwant Kaur, kills him when she finds him unable to make love to her. She is sure he has been with another women. As he gasps for breath, he tells her of the chilling experience that has rendered him impotent. 'The Assignment' is set in Amritsar. The time is 1947. A retired Muslim judge, who is alone with his teenage daughter and dying, is visited by the son of an old Sikh acquaintance for whom he had once done a favour. To acknowledge his debt, the Sikh sends him a present of food every year on the occasion of the Muslim festival of Id. When the Sikh dies, his last request to his son is that he should continue the tradition. The young man comes to the city, which is in the grip of communal riots, and finds a group of men about to attack the judge's house. He begs them to let him leave the small gift he is carrying in deference to his father's last wish. After he has completed his assignment, he tells the waiting men who are on the rampage to complete theirs.

In 'The Dutiful Daughter', an old and distraught woman looks in vain for her daughter who has been abducted. The girl has since married the man, a Sikh, who had abducted her. When she sees her mother, she refuses to recognize her. In 'Mozail', we meet a Jewish girl living in Bombay with whom a young Sikh has fallen in love 'up to his knees'. She lays down her life during the communal riots to save her lover and his bride, from his village in the Punjab. 'The Woman in the Red Coat' tells the story of an over-the-hill Anglo-Indian principal of an arts college, who is waylaid by a young man as she is trying to escape the city. He brings her to his house and as he prepares to make love to her—the entire action takes place in the dark—he realizes to his utter horror that she is not a young but an old woman. He lets her go in a storm where she meets with an accident and dies.

'The Dog of Titwal' and 'The Last Salute' relate to the war in Kashmir, months after Partition. In the first story, bored soldiers whose one link with normalcy is a dog, a pet of both sides, decide one day to amuse themselves by firing at the animal while he is trying to amble across. They end up killing the terrified animal in cold blood. In the second story, two men fighting in Kashmir—one for India, the other for Pakistan—realize that during the Second World War, they were in the same regiment and were also the best of friends. Now they belong to the two newly-independent states that are at war and so, in effect, are they. They shout to each other across the dividing line and exchange jokes and call each other by their old nicknames. But their nostalgic reunion ends in tragedy as they find themselves in an armed clash in which one of them is killed by a bullet fired by his best friend. As he lies dying, through failing eyes he sees his old senior, a captain on the Pakistani side. With superhuman willpower, the half delirious soldier lifts his arm and salutes the officer who is now an enemy but was once his superior.

In 1997, India and Pakistan celebrated the fiftieth anniversary of their Independence. Had Manto been alive, he would have pointed out that there was little to celebrate. What did they have to show for half a century of freedom? They had fought three wars and their relations were worse than they were when the British packed up and went home. There is little trade between the two and their citizens are not free to travel to each other's country except under the most stringent restrictions. The two have a population of nearly a billion people but it is not the eradication of poverty, hunger, disease and illiteracy to which their resources have been diverted, but principally to the raising of armies and the acquisition of lethal weaponry, not excluding nuclear.

Saadat Hasan Manto would not have celebrated. Perhaps that should make us all, on both sides of the long line that divides us, pause and think. The fifty pieces that constitute this book document in a powerful and moving way Manto's humanism and his conviction that happiness does not necessarily lie in conflicts over religion and nationalism, but on fellowship and caring, on love and decency, on tolerance and forgiveness. Never were these qualities more needed in the subcontinent than they are today. If Saadat Hasan Manto, who hated didacticism, were asked if he had a message for the people of the subcontinent, he would surely say, 'Yes, make peace.'

December 1996
Washington

TOBA TEK SINGH

A couple of years after the partition of the country, it occurred to the respective governments of India and Pakistan that inmates of lunatic asylums, like prisoners, should also be exchanged. Muslim lunatics in India should be transferred to Pakistan and Hindu and Sikh lunatics in Pakistani asylums should be sent to India.

Whether this was a reasonable or an unreasonable idea is difficult to say. One thing, however, is clear. It took many conferences of important officials from the two sides to come to the decision. Final details, like the date of actual exchange, were carefully worked out. Muslim lunatics whose families were still residing in India were to be left undisturbed, the rest moved to the border for the exchange. The situation in Pakistan was slightly different, since almost the entire population of Hindus and Sikhs had already migrated to India. The question of keeping non-Muslim lunatics in Pakistan did not, therefore, arise.

While it is not known what the reaction in India was, when the news reached the Lahore lunatic asylum, it immediately became the subject of heated discussion. One Muslim lunatic, a regular reader of the fire-eating daily newspaper *Zamindar*, when asked what Pakistan was, replied after deep reflection, 'The name of a place in India where cut-throat razors are manufactured.'

This profound observation was received with visible satisfaction.

A Sikh lunatic asked another Sikh, 'Sardarji, why are we being sent to India? We don't even know the language they speak in that country.'

The man smiled. 'I know the language of the Hindostoras. These devils always strut about as if they were the lords of the earth.'

One day a Muslim lunatic, while taking his bath, raised the slogan 'Pakistan Zindabad' with such enthusiasm that he lost his balance and was later found lying on the floor unconscious.

Not all inmates were mad. Some were perfectly normal, except that they were murderers. To spare them the hangman's noose, their families had managed to get them committed after bribing officials down the line. They probably had a vague idea why India was being divided and what Pakistan was, but, as for the present situation, they were equally clueless.

Newspapers were no help either, and the asylum guards were ignorant, if not illiterate. Nor was there anything to be learnt by eavesdropping on their conversations. Some said there was this man by the name Muhammad Ali Jinnah, or the Quaid-e-Azam, who had set up a separate country for Muslims, called Pakistan.

As to where Pakistan was located, the inmates knew nothing. That was why both the mad and the partially mad were unable to decide whether they were now in India or in Pakistan. If they were in India, where on earth was Pakistan? And if they were in Pakistan, then how come until only the other day it was India?

One inmate had got so badly caught up in this India–Pakistan–Pakistan–India rigmarole that one day, while sweeping the floor, he dropped everything, climbed the nearest tree and installed himself on a branch, from which vantage point he spoke for two hours on the delicate problem of India and Pakistan. The guards asked him to get down; instead he went a branch higher, and when threatened with punishment, declared, 'I wish to live neither in India nor in Pakistan. I wish to live in this tree.'

When he was finally persuaded to come down, he began embracing his Sikh and Hindu friends, tears running down his cheeks, fully convinced that they were about to leave him and go to India.

A Muslim radio engineer, who had an MSc degree, and never mixed with anyone, given as he was to taking long walks by himself all day, was so affected by the current debate that one day he took off all his clothes, gave the bundle to one of the attendants and ran into the garden stark naked.

A Muslim lunatic from Chaniot, who used to be one of the most devoted workers of the All India Muslim League, and was obsessed with bathing himself fifteen or sixteen times a day, had suddenly stopped doing that and announced his name was Muhammad Ali—that he was Quaid-e-Azam Muhammad Ali Jinnah. This had led a Sikh inmate to declare himself Master Tara Singh, the leader of the Sikhs. Apprehending serious communal trouble, the authorities declared them dangerous, and shut them up in separate cells.

There was a young Hindu lawyer from Lahore who had gone off his head after an unhappy love affair. When told that Amritsar was to become a part of India, he went into depression because his beloved lived in Amritsar, something he had not forgotten even in his madness. That day he abused every major and minor Hindu and Muslim leader who had cut India into two, turning his beloved into an Indian and him into a Pakistani.

When news of the exchange reached the asylum, his friends offered him congratulations, because he was now to be sent to India, the country of his beloved. However, he declared that he had no intention of leaving Lahore, because his practice would not flourish in Amritsar.

There were two Anglo-Indian lunatics in the European ward. When told that the British had decided to go home after granting independence to India, they went into a state of deep shock and were seen conferring with each other in whispers the entire afternoon. They were worried about their changed status after independence. Would there be a European ward or would it be abolished? Would breakfast continue to be served or would they have to subsist on bloody Indian chapatti?

There was another inmate, a Sikh, who had been confined for the last fifteen years. Whenever he spoke, it was the same mysterious gibberish: '*Uper the gur gur the annexe the bay dhayana the mung the dal of the laltain.*' Guards said he had not slept a wink in fifteen years. Occasionally, he could be observed leaning against a wall, but the rest of the time, he was always to be found standing. Because of this, his legs were permanently swollen, something that did not appear to bother him. Recently, he had started to listen carefully to discussions about the forthcoming exchange of Indian and Pakistani lunatics. When asked his opinion, he observed solemnly, '*Uper the gur gur the annexe the bay dhayana the mung the dal of the Government of Pakistan.*'

Of late, however, the Government of Pakistan had been replaced by the government of Toba Tek Singh, a small town in the Punjab which was his home. He had also begun inquiring where Toba Tek Singh was to go. However, nobody was quite sure whether it was in India or Pakistan.

Those who had tried to solve this mystery had become utterly confused when told that Sialkot, which used to be in India, was now in Pakistan. It was anybody's guess what was going to happen to Lahore, which was currently in Pakistan, but could slide into India any moment. It was also possible that the entire subcontinent of India might become Pakistan. And who could say if both India and Pakistan might not entirely vanish from the map of the world one day?

The old man's hair was almost gone and what little was left had become a part of the beard, giving him a strange, even frightening, appearance. However, he was a harmless fellow and had never been known to get into fights. Older attendants at the asylum said that he was a fairly prosperous landlord from Toba Tek Singh, who had quite suddenly gone mad. His family had brought him in, bound and fettered. That was fifteen years ago.

Once a month, he used to have visitors but, since the start of communal troubles in the Punjab, they had stopped coming. His real name was Bishen Singh, but everybody called him Toba Tek Singh. He lived in a kind of limbo, having no idea what day of the week it was, or month, or how many years had passed since his confinement. However, he had developed a sixth sense about the day of the visit, when he would bathe himself, soap his body, oil and comb his hair and put on clean clothes. He never said a word during these meetings, except occasional outbursts of, '*Uper the gur gur the annexe the bay dhayana the mung the dal of the laltain.*'

When he was first confined, he had left an infant daughter

behind, now a pretty, young girl of fifteen. She would come occasionally, and sit in front of him with tears rolling down her cheeks. In the strange world that he inhabited, hers was just another face.

Since the start of this India–Pakistan caboodle, he had got into the habit of asking fellow inmates where exactly Toba Tek Singh was, without receiving a satisfactory answer, because nobody knew. The visits had also suddenly stopped. He was increasingly restless, but, more than that, curious. The sixth sense, which used to alert him to the day of the visit, had also atrophied.

He missed his family, the gifts they used to bring and the concern with which they used to speak to him. He was sure they would have told him whether Toba Tek Singh was in India or Pakistan. He also had a feeling that they came from Toba Tek Singh, where he used to have his home.

One of the inmates had declared himself God. Bishen Singh asked him one day if Toba Tek Singh was in India or Pakistan. The man chuckled. 'Neither in India nor in Pakistan, because, so far, we have issued no orders in this respect.'

Bishen Singh begged 'God' to issue the necessary orders so that his problem could be solved, but he was disappointed, as 'God' appeared to be preoccupied with more pressing matters. Finally, he told him angrily, *'Uper the gur gur the annexe the mung the dal of Guruji da Khalsa and Guruji ki fateh . . . jo boley so nihal sat sri akal.'*

What he wanted to say was, 'You don't answer my prayers because you are a Muslim god. Had you been a Sikh god, you would have been more of a sport.'

A few days before the exchange was to take place, one of Bishen Singh's Muslim friends from Toba Tek Singh came to see him—the first time in fifteen years. Bishen Singh looked at him once and turned away, until a guard said to him, 'This is your old friend Fazal Din. He has come all the way to meet you.'

Bishen Singh looked at Fazal Din and began to mumble something. Fazal Din placed his hand on his friend's shoulder and said, 'I have been meaning to come for some time to bring you news. All your family is well and has gone to India safely.

I did what I could to help. Your daughter Roop Kaur . . .'—he hesitated—'She is safe too . . . in India.'

Bishen Singh kept quiet; Fazal Din continued, 'Your family wanted me to make sure you were well. Soon you will be moving to India. What can I say, except that you should remember me to bhai Balbir Singh, bhai Vadhawa Singh and bahain Amrit Kaur. Tell bhai Balbir Singh that Fazal Din is well by the grace of God. The two brown buffaloes he left behind are well too. Both of them gave birth to calves, but, unfortunately, one of them died after six days. Say I think of them often and to write to me if there is anything I can do.'

Then he added, 'Here, I brought you a nice treat from home.'

Bishen Singh took the gift and handed it to one of the guards. 'Where is Toba Tek Singh?' he asked.

'Where? Why, it is where it has always been.'

'In India or in Pakistan?'

'In India . . . no, in Pakistan.'

Without saying another word, Bishen Singh walked away, murmuring, *'Uper the gur gur the annexe the bay dhayana the mung the dal of the Pakistan and Hindustan dur fittay moun.'*

Meanwhile, the exchange arrangements were rapidly being finalized. Lists of lunatics from the two sides had been exchanged between the governments, and the date of transfer fixed.

On a cold winter evening, buses full of Hindu and Sikh lunatics, accompanied by armed police and officials, began moving out of the Lahore asylum towards Wagha, the dividing line between India and Pakistan. Senior officials from the two sides in charge of exchange arrangements met, signed documents and the transfer got under way.

It was quite a job getting the men out of the buses and handing them over to officials. Some just refused to leave. Those who were persuaded to do so began to run pell-mell in every direction. Some were stark naked. All efforts to get them to cover themselves had failed because they couldn't be kept from tearing off their garments. Some were shouting abuse or singing. Others were weeping bitterly. Many fights broke out.

In short, complete confusion prevailed. Female lunatics were also being exchanged and they were even noisier. It was bitterly cold.

Most of the inmates appeared to be dead set against the entire operation. They simply could not understand why they were being forcibly removed, thrown into buses and driven to this strange place. There were slogans of 'Pakistan Zindabad' and 'Pakistan Murdabad', followed by fights.

When Bishen Singh was brought out and asked to give his name so that it could be recorded in a register, he asked the official behind the desk, 'Where is Toba Tek Singh? In India or Pakistan?'

'Pakistan,' he answered with a vulgar laugh.

Bishen Singh tried to run, but was overpowered by the Pakistani guards who tried to push him across the dividing line towards India. However, he wouldn't move. 'This is Toba Tek Singh,' he announced. *'Uper the gur gur the annexe the bay dhayana mung the dal of Toba Tek Singh and Pakistan.'*

Many efforts were made to explain to him that Toba Tek Singh had already been moved to India, or would be moved immediately, but it had no effect on Bishen Singh. The guards even tried force, but soon gave up.

There he stood in no-man's-land on his swollen legs like a colossus.

Since he was a harmless old man, no further attempt was made to push him into India. He was allowed to stand where he wanted, while the exchange continued. The night wore on.

Just before sunrise, Bishen Singh, the man who had stood on his legs for fifteen years, screamed and as officials from the two sides rushed towards him, he collapsed to the ground.

There, behind barbed wire, on one side, lay India and behind more barbed wire, on the other side, lay Pakistan. In between, on a bit of earth, which had no name, lay Toba Tek Singh.

THE RETURN

The special train left Amritsar at two in the afternoon, arriving at Mughalpura, Lahore, eight hours later. Many had been killed on the way, a lot more injured and countless lost.

It was at ten o'clock the next morning that Sirajuddin regained consciousness. He was lying on bare ground, surrounded by screaming men, women and children. It did not make sense.

He lay very still, gazing at the dusty sky. He appeared not to notice the confusion or the noise. To a stranger, he might have looked like an old man in deep thought, though this was not the case. He was in shock, suspended, as it were, over a bottomless pit.

Then his eyes moved and, suddenly, caught the sun. The shock brought him back to the world of living men and women. A succession of images raced through his mind. Attack . . . fire . . . escape . . . railway station . . . night . . . Sakina. He rose abruptly and began searching through the milling crowd in the refugee camp.

He spent hours looking, all the time shouting his daughter's name . . . Sakina, Sakina . . . but she was nowhere to be found.

Total confusion prevailed, with people looking for lost sons, daughters, mothers, wives. In the end Sirajuddin gave up. He sat down, away from the crowd, and tried to think clearly. Where did he part from Sakina and her mother? Then it came to him in a flash—the dead body of his wife, her stomach ripped open. It was an image that wouldn't go away.

Sakina's mother was dead. That much was certain. She had died in front of his eyes. He could hear her voice: 'Leave me where I am. Take the girl away.'

The two of them had begun to run. Sakina's dupatta had slipped to the ground and he had stopped to pick it up and she had said, 'Father, leave it.'

He could feel a bulge in his pocket. It was a length of cloth. Yes, he recognized it. It was Sakina's dupatta, but where was she?

Other details were missing. Had he brought her as far as the railway station? Had she got into the carriage with him? When the rioters had stopped the train, had they taken her with them?

All questions. There were no answers. He wished he could weep, but tears wouldn't come. He knew then that he needed help.

A few days later, he had a break. There were eight of them, young men armed with guns. They also had a truck. They said they brought back women and children left behind on the other side.

He gave them a description of his daughter. 'She is fair, very pretty. No, she doesn't look like me, but her mother. About seventeen. Big eyes, black hair, a mole on the left cheek. Find my daughter. May God bless you.'

The young men had said to Sirajuddin, 'If your daughter is alive we will find her.'

And they had tried. At the risk of their lives, they had driven to Amritsar, recovered many women and children and brought them back to the camp, but they had not found Sakina.

On their next trip out, they had found a girl on the roadside. They seemed to have scared her and she had started running. They had stopped the truck, jumped out and run after her. Finally, they had caught up with her in a field. She was very pretty and she had a mole on her left cheek. One of the men had said to her, 'Don't be frightened. Is your name Sakina?' Her face had gone pale, but when they told her who they were she had confessed that she was Sakina, daughter of Sirajuddin.

The young men were very kind to her. They had fed her, given her milk to drink and put her in their truck. One of them had given her his jacket so that she could cover herself. It was obvious that she was ill at ease without her dupatta, trying nervously to cover her breasts with her arms.

Many days had gone by and Sirajuddin had still not had any news of his daughter. All his time was spent running from camp to camp, looking for her. At night, he would pray for the success of the young men who were looking for his daughter. Their words would ring in his ears: 'If your daughter is alive, we will find her.'

Then one day he saw them in the camp. They were about to drive away. 'Son,' he shouted after one of them, 'have you found Sakina, my daughter?'

'We will, we will,' they replied all together.

The old man again prayed for them. It made him feel better.

That evening there was sudden activity in the camp. He saw four men carrying the body of a young girl found unconscious near the railway tracks. They were taking her to the camp hospital. He began to follow them.

He stood outside the hospital for some time, then went in. In one of the rooms, he found a stretcher with someone lying on it.

A light was switched on. It was a young woman with a mole on her left cheek. 'Sakina,' Sirajuddin screamed.

The doctor, who had switched on the light, stared at Sirajuddin.

'I am her father,' he stammered.

The doctor looked at the prostrate body and felt for the pulse. Then he said to the old man, pointing at the window, 'Open it.'

The young woman on the stretcher moved slightly. Her hands groped for the cord that kept her shalwar tied round her waist. With painful slowness, she unfastened it, pulled the garment down and opened her thighs.

'She is alive. My daughter is alive,' Sirajuddin shouted with joy.

The doctor broke into a cold sweat.

THE ASSIGNMENT

Beginning with isolated incidents of stabbing, it had now developed into full-scale communal violence, with no holds barred. Even home-made bombs were being used.

The general view in Amritsar was that the riots could not last long. They were seen as no more than a manifestation of temporarily inflamed political passions which were bound to cool down before long. After all, these were not the first communal riots the city had known. There had been so many of them in the past. They never lasted long. The pattern was familiar. Two weeks or so of unrest and then business as usual. On the basis of experience, therefore, the people were quite justified in believing that the current troubles would also run their course in a few days. But this did not happen. They not only continued, but grew in intensity.

Muslims living in Hindu localities began to leave for safer places, and Hindus in Muslim majority areas followed suit. However, everyone saw these adjustments as strictly temporary. The atmosphere would soon be clear of this communal madness, they told themselves.

Retired judge Mian Abdul Hai was absolutely confident that things would return to normal soon, which was why he wasn't worried. He had two children, a boy of eleven and a girl of seventeen. In addition, there was an old servant who was now pushing seventy. It was a small family. When the troubles started, Mian sahib, being an extra cautious man, had stocked up on food . . . just in case. So on one count, at least, there were no worries.

His daughter, Sughra, was less sure of things. They lived in a three-storey house with a view of almost the entire city. Sughra could not help noticing that, whenever she went on the roof, there were fires raging everywhere. In the beginning, she could hear fire engines rushing past, their bells ringing, but this had now stopped. There were too many fires in too many places.

The nights had become particularly frightening. The sky was always lit by conflagrations like giants spitting out flames. Then there were the slogans that rent the air with terrifying frequency—'Allaho Akbar', 'Har Har Mahadev'.

Sughra never expressed her fears to her father, because he had declared confidently that there was no cause for anxiety. Everything was going to be fine. Since he was generally always right, she had initially felt reassured.

However, when the power and water supplies were suddenly cut off, she expressed her unease to her father and suggested apologetically that, for a few days at least, they should move to Sharifpura, a Muslim locality, where many of the old residents had already moved to. Mian sahib was adamant. 'You're imagining things. Everything is going to be normal very soon.'

He was wrong. Things went from bad to worse. Before long there was not a single Muslim family to be found in Mian Abdul Hai's locality. Then one day Mian sahib suffered a stroke and was laid up in bed. His son, Basharat, who used to spend most of his time playing self-devised games, now stayed glued to his father's bed.

All the shops in the area had been permanently boarded up. Dr Ghulam Hussain's dispensary had been shut for weeks and Sughra had noticed from the rooftop one day that the adjoining clinic of Dr Goranditta Mal was also closed. Mian sahib's condition was getting worse day by day. Sughra was almost at her wits' end. One day she took Basharat aside and said to him, 'You've got to do something. I know it's not safe to go out, but we must get some help. Our father is very ill.'

The boy went, but came back almost immediately. His face was pale with fear. He had seen a blood-drenched body lying in the street and a group of wild-looking men looting shops. Sughra took the terrified boy in her arms and said a silent prayer, thanking God for his safe return. However, she could not bear her father's suffering. His left side was now completely lifeless. His speech had been impaired and he mostly communicated through gestures, all designed to reassure Sughra that soon all would be well.

It was the month of Ramadan and only two days to Id. Mian sahib was quite confident that the troubles would be over by then. He was again wrong. A canopy of smoke hung over the city, with fires burning everywhere. At night the silence was shattered by deafening explosions. Sughra and Basharat hadn't slept for days.

Sughra in any case couldn't because of her father's deteriorating condition. Helplessly, she would look at him, then at her young, frightened brother and the seventy-year-old servant Akbar, who was useless for all practical purposes. He mostly kept to his bed, coughing and fighting for breath. One day Sughra told him angrily, 'What good are you? Do you realize how ill Mian sahib is? Perhaps you are too lazy to want to help, pretending that you are suffering from acute asthma. There was a time when servants used to sacrifice their lives for their masters.'

Sughra felt very bad afterwards. She had been unnecessarily harsh on the old man. In the evening, when she took his food to him in his small room, he was not there. Basharat looked for him all over the house, but he was nowhere to be found. The front door was unlatched. He was gone, perhaps to get some help for Mian sahib. Sughra prayed for his return, but two days passed and he hadn't come back.

It was evening and the festival of Id was now only a day away. She remembered the excitement that used to grip the family on this occasion. She remembered standing on the rooftop, peering into the sky, looking for the Id moon and praying for the clouds to clear. But how different everything was today. The sky was covered in smoke and on distant roofs one could see people looking upwards. Were they trying to catch sight of the new moon or were they watching the fires, she wondered.

She looked up and saw the thin sliver of the moon peeping through a small patch in the sky. She raised her hands in prayer, begging God to make her father well. Basharat, however, was upset that there would be no Id this year.

The night hadn't yet fallen. Sughra had moved her father's bed out of the room on to the veranda. She was sprinkling water on the floor to make it cool. Mian sahib was lying there quietly, looking with vacant eyes at the sky where she had seen the moon. Sughra came and sat next to him. He motioned her to get closer. Then he raised his right hand slowly and put it on her head. Tears began to run from Sughra's eyes. Even Mian sahib looked moved. Then with great difficulty he said to her, 'God is merciful. All will be well.'

Suddenly there was a knock on the door. Sughra's heart began to beat violently. She looked at Basharat, whose face had turned white like a sheet of paper. There was another knock. Mian sahib gestured to Sughra to answer it. It must be old Akbar who had come back, she thought. She said to Basharat, 'Answer the door. I'm sure it's Akbar.' Her father shook his head, as if to signal disagreement.

'Then who can it be?' Sughra asked him.

Mian Abdul Hai tried to speak, but before he could do so Basharat came running in. He was breathless. Taking Sughra aside, he whispered, 'It's a Sikh.'

Sughra screamed, 'A Sikh! What does he want?'

'He wants me to open the door.'

Sughra took Basharat in her arms and went and sat on her father's bed, looking at him desolately.

On Mian Abdul Hai's thin, lifeless lips, a faint smile appeared. 'Go and open the door. It is Gurmukh Singh.'

'No, it's someone else,' Basharat said.

Mian sahib turned to Sughra. 'Open the door. It's him.'

Sughra rose. She knew Gurmukh Singh. Her father had once done him a favour. He had been involved in a false legal suit and Mian sahib had acquitted him. That was a long time ago, but every year, on the occasion of Id, he would come all the way from his village with a bag of sawwaiyaan. Mian sahib had told him several times, 'Sardar sahib, you really are too kind. You shouldn't inconvenience yourself every year.' But Gurmukh Singh would always reply, 'Mian sahib, God has given you everything. This is only a small gift that I bring every year in humble acknowledgement of the kindness you did me once. Even a hundred generations of mine would not be able to repay your favour. May God keep you happy.'

Sughra was reassured. Why hadn't she thought of it in the first place? But why had Basharat said it was someone else? After all, he knew Gurmukh Singh's face from his annual visit.

Sughra went to the front door. There was another knock. Her heart missed a beat. 'Who is it?' she asked in a faint voice.

Basharat whispered to her to look through a small hole in the door.

It wasn't Gurmukh Singh, who was a very old man. This was a young fellow. He knocked again. He was holding a bag in his hand of the same kind Gurmukh Singh used to bring.

'Who are you?' she asked, a little more confident now.

'I am Sardar Gurmukh Singh's son Santokh.'

Sughra's fear had suddenly gone. 'What brings you here today?' she asked politely.

'Where is Judge sahib?' he asked.

'He is not well,' Sughra answered.

'Oh, I'm sorry,' Santokh Singh said. Then he shifted his bag from one hand to the other. 'Here is some sawwaiyaan.' Then after a pause, 'Sardarji is dead.'

'Dead!'

'Yes, a month ago, but one of the last things he said to me was, "For the last ten years, on the occasion of Id, I have always taken my small gift to Judge sahib. After I am gone, it will become your duty." I gave him my word that I would not fail him. I am here today to honour the promise made to my father on his deathbed.'

Sughra was so moved that tears came to her eyes. She opened the door a little. The young man pushed the bag towards her. 'May God rest his soul,' she said.

'Is Judge sahib not well?' he asked.

'No.'

'What's wrong?'

'He had a stroke.'

'Had my father been alive, it would have grieved him deeply. He never forgot Judge sahib's kindness until his last breath. He used to say, "He is not a man, but a god." May God keep him under his care. Please convey my respects to him.'

He left before Sughra could make up her mind whether or not to ask him to get a doctor.

As Santokh Singh turned the corner, four men, their faces covered with their turbans, moved towards him. Two of them held burning oil torches; the others carried cans of kerosene oil and explosives. One of them asked Santokh, 'Sardarji, have you completed your assignment?'

The young man nodded.

'Should we then proceed with ours?' he asked.

'If you like,' he replied and walked away.

COLDER THAN ICE

As Ishwar Singh entered the room, Kalwant Kaur rose from the bed and locked the door from the inside. It was past midnight. A strange and ominous silence seemed to have descended on the city.

Kalwant Kaur returned to the bed, crossed her legs and sat down in the middle. Ishwar Singh stood quietly in a corner, holding his kirpan absent-mindedly. Anxiety and confusion were writ large on his handsome face.

Kalwant Kaur, apparently dissatisfied with her defiant posture, moved to the edge and sat down, swinging her legs suggestively. Ishwar Singh still had not spoken.

Kalwant Kaur was a big woman with generous hips, fleshy thighs and unusually high breasts. Her eyes were sharp and bright and over her upper lip there was faint bluish down. Her chin suggested great strength and resolution.

Ishwar Singh had not moved from his corner. His turban, which he always kept smartly in place, was loose and his hands trembled from time to time. However, from his strapping, manly figure, it was apparent that he had just what it took to be Kalwant Kaur's lover.

More time passed. Kalwant Kaur was getting restive. 'Ishr Sian,' she said in a sharp voice.

Ishwar Singh raised his head, then turned it away, unable to deal with Kalwant Kaur's fiery gaze.

This time she screamed, 'Ishr Sian.' Then she lowered her voice and added, 'Where have you been all this time?'

Ishwar Singh moistened his parched lips and said, 'I don't know.'

Kalwant Kaur lost her temper. 'What sort of a motherfucking answer is that!'

Ishwar Singh threw his kirpan aside and slumped on the bed. He looked unwell. She stared at him and her anger seemed to have left her. Putting her hand on his forehead, she asked gently, 'Jani, what's wrong?'

'Kalwant.' He turned his gaze from the ceiling and looked at her. There was pain in his voice and it melted all of Kalwant Kaur. She bit her lower lip. 'Yes jani.'

Ishwar Singh took off his turban. He slapped her thigh and said, more to himself than to her, 'I feel strange.'

His long hair came undone and Kalwant Kaur began to run her fingers through it playfully. 'Ishr Sian, where have you been all this time?'

'In the bed of my enemy's mother,' he said jocularly. Then he pulled Kalwant Kaur towards him and began to knead her breasts with both hands. 'I swear by the Guru, there's no other woman like you.'

Flirtatiously, she pushed him aside. 'Swear over my head. Did you go to the city?'

He gathered his hair in a bun and replied, 'No.'

Kalwant Kaur was irritated. 'Yes, you did go to the city and you looted a lot more money and you don't want to tell me about it.'

'May I not be my father's son if I lie to you,' he said.

She was silent for a while, then she exploded, 'Tell me what happened to you the last night you were here. You were lying next to me and you had made me wear all those gold ornaments you had looted from the houses of the Muslims in the city and you were kissing me all over and then, suddenly, God only knows what came over you, you put on your clothes and walked out.'

Ishwar Singh went pale. 'See how your face has fallen,' Kalwant Kaur snapped. 'Ishr Sian,' she said, emphasizing every word, 'you're not the man you were eight days ago. Something has happened.'

Ishwar Singh did not answer, but he was stung. He suddenly took Kalwant Kaur in his arms and began to hug and kiss her ferociously. 'Jani, I'm what I always was. Squeeze me tighter so that the heat in your bones cools off.'

Kalwant Kaur did not resist him, but she kept asking, 'What went wrong that night?'

'Nothing.'

'Why don't you tell me?'

'There's nothing to tell.'

'Ishr Sian, may you cremate my body with your own hands if you lie to me!'

Ishwar Singh did not reply. He dug his lips into hers. His moustache tickled her nostrils and she sneezed. They burst out laughing.

Ishwar Singh began to take off his clothes, ogling Kalwant Kaur lasciviously. 'It's time for a game of cards.'

Beads of perspiration appeared over her upper lip. She rolled her eyes coquettishly and said, 'Get lost.'

Ishwar Singh pinched her lip and she leapt aside. 'Ishr Sian, don't do that. It hurts.'

Ishwar Singh began to suck her lower lip and Kalwant Kaur melted. He took off the rest of his clothes. 'Time for a round of trumps,' he said.

Kalwant Kaur's upper lip began to quiver. He peeled her shirt off, as if he was skinning a banana. He fondled her naked body and pinched her arm. 'Kalwant, I swear by the Guru, you're not a woman, you're a delicacy,' he said between kisses.

Kalwant Kaur examined the skin he had pinched. It was red. 'Ishr Sian, you're a brute.'

Ishwar Singh smiled through his thick moustache. 'Then let there be a lot of brutality tonight.' And he began to prove what he had said.

He bit her lower lip, nibbled at her earlobes, kneaded her breasts, slapped her glowing hip resoundingly and planted big, wet kisses on her cheeks.

Kalwant Kaur began to boil with passion like a kettle on high fire.

But there was something wrong.

Ishwar Singh, despite his vigorous efforts at foreplay, could not feel the fire which leads to the final and inevitable act of love. Like a wrestler who is being had the better of, he employed every trick he knew to ignite the fire in his loins, but it eluded him. He felt cold.

Kalwant Kaur was now like an overtuned instrument. 'Ishr Sian,' she whispered languidly, 'you have shuffled me enough, it is time to produce your trump.'

Ishwar Singh felt as if the entire deck of cards had slipped from his hands on to the floor.

He laid himself against her, breathing irregularly. Drops of cold perspiration appeared on his brow. Kalwant Kaur made frantic efforts to arouse him, but in the end she gave up.

In a fury, she sprang out of bed and covered herself with a sheet. 'Ishr Sian, tell me the name of the bitch you have been with who has squeezed you dry.'

Ishwar Singh just lay there panting.

'Who was that bitch?' she screamed.

'No one, Kalwant, no one,' he replied in a barely audible voice.

Kalwant Kaur placed her hands on her hips. 'Ishr Sian, I'm going to get to the bottom of this. Swear to me on the Guru's sacred name, is there a woman?'

She did not let him speak. 'Before you swear by the Guru, don't forget who I am. I am Sardar Nihal Singh's daughter. I will cut you to pieces. Is there a woman in this?'

He nodded his head in assent, his pain obvious from his face.

Like a wild and demented creature, Kalwant Kaur picked up Ishwar Singh's kirpan, unsheathed it and plunged it in his neck. Blood spluttered out of the deep gash like water out of a fountain. Then she began to pull at his hair and scratch his face, cursing her unknown rival as she continued tearing at him.

'Let go, Kalwant, let go now,' Ishwar Singh begged.

She paused. His beard and chest were drenched in blood. 'You acted impetuously,' he said, 'but what you did I deserved.'

'Tell me the name of that woman of yours,' she screamed.

A thin line of blood ran into his mouth. He shivered as he felt its taste.

'Kalwant, with this kirpan I have killed six men . . . with this kirpan with which you . . .'

'Who was the bitch, I ask you?' she repeated.

Ishwar Singh's dimming eyes sparked into momentary life. 'Don't call her a bitch,' he implored.

'Who was she?' she screamed.

Ishwar Singh's voice was failing. 'I'll tell you.' He ran his hand over his throat, then looked at it, smiling wanly. 'What a motherfucking creature man is!'

'Ishr Sian, answer my question,' Kalwant Kaur said.

He began to speak, very slowly, his face coated with cold sweat.

'Kalwant, jani, you can have no idea what happened to me. When they began to loot Muslim shops and houses in the city, I joined one of the gangs. All the cash and ornaments that fell to my share, I brought back to you. There was only one thing I hid from you.'

He began to groan. His pain was becoming unbearable, but she was unconcerned. 'Go on,' she said in a merciless voice.

'There was this house I broke into . . . there were seven people in there, six of them men whom I killed with my kirpan one by one . . . and there was one girl . . . she was so beautiful . . . I didn't kill her . . . I took her away.'

She sat on the edge of the bed, listening to him.

'Kalwant jani, I can't even begin to describe to you how beautiful she was . . . I could have slashed her throat but I didn't . . . I said to myself . . . Ishr Sian, you gorge yourself on Kalwant Kaur every day . . . how about a mouthful of this luscious fruit!

'I thought she had gone into a faint, so I carried her over my shoulder all the way to the canal which runs outside the city . . . then I laid her down on the grass, behind some bushes and . . . first I thought I would shuffle her a bit . . . but then I decided to trump her right away . . .'

'What happened?' she asked.

'I threw the trump . . . but, but . . .'

His voice sank.

Kalwant Kaur shook him violently. 'What happened?'

Ishwar Singh opened his eyes. 'She was dead . . . I had carried a dead body . . . a heap of cold flesh . . . jani, give me your hand.'

Kalwant Kaur placed her hand on his. It was colder than ice.

THE DOG OF TITWAL

The soldiers had been entrenched in their positions for several weeks, but there was little, if any, fighting, except for the dozen rounds they ritually exchanged every day. The weather was extremely pleasant. The air was heavy with the scent of wild flowers and nature seemed to be following its course, quite unmindful of the soldiers hiding behind rocks and camouflaged by mountain shrubbery. The birds sang as they always had and the flowers were in bloom. Bees buzzed about lazily.

Only when a shot rang out, the birds got startled and took flight, as if a musician had struck a jarring note on his instrument. It was almost the end of September, neither hot nor cold. It seemed as if summer and winter had made their peace. In the blue skies, cotton clouds floated all day like barges on a lake.

The soldiers seemed to be getting tired of this indecisive war where nothing much ever happened. Their positions were quite impregnable. The two hills on which they were placed faced each other and were about the same height, so no one side had an advantage. Down below in the valley, a stream zigzagged furiously on its stony bed like a snake.

The air force was not involved in the combat and neither of the adversaries had heavy guns or mortars. At night, they would light huge fires and hear each others' voices echoing through the hills.

The last round of tea had just been taken. The fire had gone cold. The sky was clear and there was a chill in the air and a sharp, though not unpleasant, smell of pine cones. Most of the soldiers were already asleep, except Jamadar Harnam Singh, who was on night watch. At two o'clock, he woke up Ganda Singh to take over. Then he lay down, but sleep was as far away from his eyes as the stars in the sky. He began to hum a Punjabi folk song:

Buy me a pair of shoes, my lover
A pair of shoes with stars on them
Sell your buffalo, if you have to
But buy me a pair of shoes
With stars on them.

It made him feel good and a bit sentimental. He woke up the others one by one. Banta Singh, the youngest of the soldiers, who had a sweet voice, began to sing a lovelorn verse from *Heer Ranjha*, that timeless Punjabi epic of love and tragedy. A deep sadness fell over them. Even the grey hills seemed to have been affected by the melancholy of the songs.

This mood was shattered by the barking of a dog. Jamadar Harnam Singh said, 'Where has this son of a bitch materialized from?'

The dog barked again. He sounded closer. There was a rustle in the bushes. Banta Singh got up to investigate and came back with an ordinary mongrel in tow. He was wagging his tail. 'I found him behind the bushes and he told me his name was Jhun Jhun,' Banta Singh announced. Everybody burst out laughing.

The dog went to Harnam Singh, who produced a cracker from his kitbag and threw it on the ground. The dog sniffed at it and was about to eat it, when Harnam Singh snatched it away . . . 'Wait, you could be a Pakistani dog.'

They laughed. Banta Singh patted the animal and said to Harnam Singh, 'Jamadar sahib, Jhun Jhun is an Indian dog.'

'Prove your identity,' Harnam Singh ordered the dog, who began to wag his tail.

'This is no proof of identity. All dogs can wag their tails,' Harnam Singh said.

'He is only a poor refugee,' Banta Singh said, playing with his tail.

Harnam Singh threw the dog a cracker, which he caught in mid-air. 'Even dogs will now have to decide if they are Indian or Pakistani,' one of the soldiers observed.

Harnam Singh produced another cracker from his kitbag. 'And all Pakistanis, including dogs, will be shot.'

A soldier shouted, 'India Zindabad!'

The dog, who was about to munch his cracker, stopped dead in his tracks, put his tail between his legs and looked scared. Harnam Singh laughed. 'Why are you afraid of your own country? Here, Jhun Jhun, have another cracker.'

The morning broke very suddenly, as if someone had switched on a light in a dark room. It spread across the hills and valleys of Titwal, which is what the area was called.

The war had been going on for months but nobody could be quite sure who was winning it.

Jamadar Harnam Singh surveyed the area with his binoculars. He could see smoke rising from the opposite hill, which meant that, like them, the enemy was busy preparing breakfast.

Subedar Himmat Khan of the Pakistan army gave his huge moustache a twirl and began to study the map of the Titwal sector. Next to him sat his wireless operator, who was trying to establish contact with the platoon commander to obtain instructions. A few feet away, the soldier Bashir sat on the ground, his back against a rock and his rifle in front of him. He was humming:

Where did you spend the night, my love, my moon?
Where did you spend the night?

Enjoying himself, he began to sing more loudly, savouring the words. Suddenly he heard Subedar Himmat Khan scream, 'Where did *you* spend the night?'

But this was not addressed to Bashir. It was a dog he was shouting at. He had come to them from nowhere a few days ago, stayed in the camp quite happily and then suddenly disappeared last night. However, he had now returned like a bad coin.

Bashir smiled and began to sing to the dog. 'Where did *you* spend the night, where did you spend the night?' But he only wagged his tail. Subedar Himmat Khan threw a pebble at him. 'All he can do is wag his tail, the idiot.'

'What has he got around his neck?' Bashir asked.

One of the soldiers grabbed the dog and undid his makeshift

rope collar. There was a small piece of cardboard tied to it. 'What does it say?' the soldier, who could not read, asked.

Bashir stepped forward and with some difficulty was able to decipher the writing. 'It says Jhun Jhun.'

Subedar Himmat Khan gave his famous moustache another mighty twirl and said, 'Perhaps it is a code. Does it say anything else, Bashirey?'

'Yes sir, it says it is an Indian dog.'

'What does that mean?' Subedar Himmat Khan asked.

'Perhaps it is a secret,' Bashir answered seriously.

'If there is a secret, it is in the word Jhun Jhun,' another soldier ventured in a wise guess.

'You may have something there,' Subedar Himmat Khan observed.

Dutifully, Bashir read the whole thing again. 'Jhun Jhun. This is an Indian dog.'

Subedar Himmat Khan picked up the wireless set and spoke to his platoon commander, providing him with a detailed account of the dog's sudden appearance in their position, his equally sudden disappearance the night before and his return that morning. 'What are you talking about?' the platoon commander asked.

Subedar Himmat Khan studied the map again. Then he tore up a packet of cigarettes, cut a small piece from it and gave it to Bashir. 'Now write on it in Gurmukhi, the language of those Sikhs . . .'

'What should I write?'

'Well . . .'

Bashir had an inspiration. 'Shun Shun, yes, that's right. We counter Jhun Jhun with Shun Shun.'

'Good,' Subedar Himmat Khan said approvingly. 'And add: This is a Pakistani dog.'

Subedar Himmat Khan personally threaded the piece of paper through the dog's collar and said, 'Now go join your family.'

He gave him something to eat and then said, 'Look here, my friend, no treachery. The punishment for treachery is death.'

The dog kept eating his food and wagging his tail. Then Subedar Himmat Khan turned him round to face the Indian position and said, 'Go and take this message to the enemy, but come back. These are the orders of your commander.'

The dog wagged his tail and moved down the winding hilly track that led into the valley dividing the two hills. Subedar Himmat Khan picked up his rifle and fired in the air.

The Indians were a bit puzzled, as it was somewhat early in the day for that sort of thing. Jamadar Harnam Singh, who in any case was feeling bored, shouted, 'Let's give it to them.'

The two sides exchanged fire for half an hour, which of course was a complete waste of time. Finally, Jamadar Harnam Singh ordered that enough was enough. He combed his long hair, looked at himself in the mirror and asked Banta Singh, 'Where has that dog Jhun Jhun gone?'

'Dogs can never digest butter, goes the famous saying,' Banta Singh observed philosophically.

Suddenly the soldier on lookout duty shouted, 'There he comes.'

'Who?' Jamadar Harnam Singh asked.

'What was his name? Jhun Jhun,' the soldier answered.

'What is he doing?' Harnam Singh asked.

'Just coming our way,' the soldier replied, peering through his binoculars.

Subedar Harnam Singh snatched them from him. 'That's him all right and there's something around his neck. But, wait, that's the Pakistani hill he's coming from, the motherfucker.'

He picked up his rifle, aimed and fired. The bullet hit some rocks close to where the dog was. He stopped.

Subedar Himmat Khan heard the report and looked through his binoculars. The dog had turned round and was running back. 'The brave never run away from battle. Go forward and complete your mission,' he shouted at the dog. To scare him, he fired at the same time. The bullet passed within inches of the dog, who leapt in the air, flapping his ears. Subedar Himmat Khan fired again, hitting some stones.

It soon became a game between the two soldiers, with the dog running round in circles in a state of great terror. Both Himmat Khan and Harnam Singh were laughing boisterously. The dog began to run towards Harnam Singh, who abused him loudly and fired. The bullet caught him in the leg. He yelped, turned around and began to run towards Himmat Khan, only to meet more fire, which was only meant to scare him. 'Be a brave boy. If you are injured, don't let that stand between you and your duty. Go, go, go,' the Pakistani shouted.

The dog turned. One of his legs was now quite useless. He began to drag himself towards Harnam Singh, who picked up his rifle, aimed carefully and shot him dead.

Subedar Himmat Khan sighed, 'The poor bugger has been martyred.'

Jamadar Harnam Singh ran his hand over the still-hot barrel of his rifle and muttered, 'He died a dog's death.'

THE LAST SALUTE

This Kashmir war was a very odd affair. Subedar Rab Nawaz often felt as if his brain had turned into a rifle with a faulty safety catch.

He had fought with distinction on many major fronts in the Second World War. He was respected by both his seniors and his juniors because of his intelligence and valour. He was always given the most difficult and dangerous assignments and he had never failed the trust placed in him.

But he had never been in a war like this one. He had come to it full of enthusiasm and with the itch to fight and liquidate the enemy. However, the first encounter had shown that the men arrayed against them on the other side were mostly old friends and comrades with whom he had fought in the old British Indian army against the Germans and the Italians. The friends of yesterday had been transformed into the enemies of today.

At times, the whole thing felt like a dream to Subedar Rab Nawaz. He could remember the day the Second World War was declared. He had enlisted immediately. They had been given some basic training and then packed off to the front. He had been moved from one theatre of war to another and, one day, the war had ended. Then had come Pakistan and the new war he was now fighting. So much had happened in these last few years at such breakneck speed. Often it made no sense at all. Those who had planned and executed these great events had perhaps deliberately maintained a dizzying pace so that the participants would get no time to think. How else could one explain one revolution followed by another and then another?

One thing Subedar Rab Nawaz could understand. They were fighting this war to win Kashmir. Why did they want to win Kashmir? Because it was crucial to Pakistan's security and survival. However, sometimes when he sat behind a gun emplacement and caught sight of a familiar face on the other side, for a moment he forgot why they were fighting. He forgot why he was carrying a gun and killing people. At such times, he would remind himself that he was not fighting to win medals or earn a salary, but to secure the survival of his country.

This was his country before the establishment of Pakistan and it was his country now. This was his land. But now he was fighting against men who were his countrymen until only the other day. Men who had grown up in the same village, whose families had been known to his family for generations. These men had now been turned into citizens of a country to which they were complete strangers. They had been told: we are placing a gun in your hands so that you can go and fight for a country that you have yet to know, where you do not even have a roof over your head, where even the air and water are strange to you. Go and fight for it against Pakistan, the land where you were born and grew up.

Rab Nawaz would think of those Muslim soldiers who had moved to Pakistan, leaving their ancestral homes behind, and come to this new country with empty hands. They had been given nothing, except the guns that had been put in their hands. The same guns they had always used, the same make, the same bore, guns to fight their new enemy with.

Before the Partition of the country, they used to fight one common enemy who was not really their enemy, perhaps, but whom they had accepted as their enemy for the sake of employment and rewards and medals. Formerly, all of them were Indian soldiers, but now some were Indian and others were Pakistani soldiers. Rab Nawaz could not unravel this puzzle. And when he thought about Kashmir, he became even more confused. Were the Pakistani soldiers fighting for Kashmir or for the Muslims of Kashmir? If they were being asked to fight in defence of the Muslims of Kashmir, why had they not been asked to fight for the Muslims of the princely states of Junagarh and Hyderabad? And if this was an Islamic war, then why were other Muslim countries of the world not fighting shoulder to shoulder with them?

Rab Nawaz had finally come to the conclusion that such intricate and subtle matters were beyond the comprehension of a simple soldier. A soldier should be thick in the head. Only the thick-headed made good soldiers, but despite this resolution, he couldn't help wondering sometimes about the war he was now in.

The fighting in what was called the Titwal sector was spread across the Kishan Ganga river and along the road that led from Muzaffarabad to Kiran. It was a strange war. Often at night, instead of gunfire, one heard abuse being exchanged in loud voices.

One late evening, while Subedar Rab Nawaz was preparing his platoon for a foray into enemy territory, he heard loud voices from across the hill the enemy was supposed to be on. He could not believe his ears. There was loud laughter followed by abuse. 'Pig's trotters,' he murmured, 'what on earth is going on?'

One of his men returned the abuse in as loud a voice as he could muster, then complained to him, 'Subedar sahib, they are abusing us again, the motherfuckers.'

Rab Nawaz's first instinct was to join the slanging match, but he thought better of it. The men fell silent too, following his example. However, after a while, the torrent of abuse from the other side became so intolerable that his men lost control and began to match abuse with abuse. A couple of times he ordered them to keep quiet, but did not insist because, frankly, it was difficult for a human being not to react violently.

They couldn't of course see the enemy at night, and hardly did so during the day because of the hilly country, which provided perfect cover. All they heard was abuse, which echoed across the hills and valleys and then evaporated in the air.

Some of the hills were barren, while others were covered with tall pine trees. It was very difficult terrain. Subedar Rab Nawaz's platoon was on a bare, treeless hill, which provided no cover. His men were itching to go into attack to avenge the abuse, which had been hurled at them without respite for several weeks. An attack was planned and executed with success, though they lost two men and suffered four injuries. The enemy lost three and abandoned the position, leaving behind food and provisions.

Subedar Rab Nawaz and his men were sorry they had not been able to capture an enemy soldier. They could then have avenged the abuse face to face. However, they had captured an important and difficult feature. Rab Nawaz relayed the news of the victory to his commander, Major Aslam, and was commended for gallantry.

On top of most hills one found ponds. There was a large one on the hill they had captured. The water was clear and sweet and, although it was cold, they took off their clothes and jumped in. Suddenly they heard firing. They jumped out of the pond and hit the ground—naked. Subedar Rab Nawaz crawled towards his binoculars, picked them up and surveyed the area carefully. He could see no one. There was more firing. This time he was able to determine its origin. It was coming from a small hill, lying a few hundred feet below their perch. He ordered his men to open up.

The enemy troops did not have very good cover and Rab Nawaz was confident they could not stay there much longer. The moment they decided to move, they would come in direct range of their guns. Sporadic firing kept getting exchanged. Finally, Rab Nawaz ordered that no more ammunition should be wasted. They should just wait for the enemy to break cover. Then he looked at his still naked body and murmured, 'Pig's trotters. Man does look silly without clothes.'

For two whole days, this game continued. Occasional fire was exchanged, but the enemy had obviously decided to lie low. Then suddenly the temperature dropped several degrees. To keep his men warm, Subedar Rab Nawaz ordered that the tea kettle should be kept on the boil all the time. It was like an unending tea party.

On the third day—it was unbearably cold—the soldier on the lookout reported that some movement could be detected around the enemy position. Subedar Rab Nawaz looked through his binoculars. Yes, something was going on. Rab Nawaz raised his rifle and fired. Someone called his name, or so he thought. It echoed through the valley. 'Pig's trotters,' Rab Nawaz shouted, 'what do you want?'

The distance that separated their two positions was not great; the voice came back, 'Don't hurl abuse, brother.'

Rab Nawaz looked at his men. The word 'brother' seemed to hang in the air. He raised his hands to his mouth and shouted, 'Brother! There are no brothers here, only your mother's lovers.'

'Rab Nawaz,' the voice shouted.

He trembled. The words reverberated around the hills and then faded into the atmosphere.

'Pig's trotters,' he whispered, 'who was that?'

He knew that the troops in the Titwal sector were mostly from the old 6/9 Jat Regiment, his own regiment. But who was this joker shouting his name? He had many friends in the regiment, and some enemies too. But who was this man who had called him brother?

Rab Nawaz looked through his binoculars again, but could see nothing. He shouted, 'Who was that? This is Rab Nawaz. Rab Nawaz. Rab Nawaz.'

'It is me . . . Ram Singh,' the same voice answered.

Rab Nawaz nearly jumped. 'Ram Singh, oh, Ram Singha, Ram Singha, you pig's trotters.'

'Shut your trap, you potter's ass,' came the reply.

Rab Nawaz looked at his men, who appeared startled at this strange exchange in the middle of battle. 'He's talking rot, pig's trotters.' Then he shouted, 'You slaughtered swine, watch your tongue.'

Ram Singh began to laugh. Rab Nawaz could not contain himself either. His men watched him in silence.

'Look, my friend, we want to drink tea,' Ram Singh said.

'Go ahead then. Have a good time,' Rab Nawaz replied.

'We can't. The tea things are lying elsewhere.'

'Where's elsewhere?'

'Let me put it this way. If we tried to get them, you could blow us to bits. We'd have to break cover.'

'So what do you want, pig's trotters?' Rab Nawaz laughed.

'That you hold your fire until we get our things.'

'Go ahead,' Rab Nawaz said.

'You will blow us up, you potter's ass,' Ram Singh shouted.

'Shut your mouth, you crawly Sikh tortoise,' Rab Nawaz said. 'Take an oath on something that you won't open fire.'

'On what?'

'Anything you like.'

Rab Nawaz laughed. 'You have my word. Now go get your things.'

Nothing happened for a few minutes. One of the men was watching the small hill through his binoculars. He pointed at his gun and asked Rab Nawaz in gestures if he should open fire.

'No, no, no shooting,' Rab Nawaz said.

Suddenly, a man darted forward, running low towards some bushes. A few minutes later he ran back, carrying an armful of things. Then he disappeared. Rab Nawaz picked up his rifle and fired. 'Thank you,' Ram Singh's voice came.

'No mention,' Rab Nawaz answered. 'OK, boys, let's give the buggers one round.'

More by way of entertainment than war, this exchange of fire continued for some time. Rab Nawaz could see smoke going up in a thin blue spiral where the enemy was. 'Is your tea ready, Ram Singha?' he shouted.

'Not yet, you potter's ass.'

Rab Nawaz was a potter by caste and any reference to his origins always enraged him. Ram Singh was the one person who could get away with calling him a potter's ass. They had grown up together in the same village in the Punjab. They were the same age, had gone to the same primary school, and their fathers had been childhood friends. They had joined the army the same day. In the last war, they had fought together on the same fronts.

'Pig's trotters, he never gives up, that one,' Rab Nawaz said to his men. 'Shut up, lice-infested donkey Ram Singha,' he shouted.

He saw a man stand up. Rab Nawaz raised his rifle and fired in his direction. He heard a scream. He looked through his binoculars. It was Ram Singh. He was doubled up, holding his stomach. Then he fell to the ground.

Rab Nawaz shouted, 'Ram Singh' and stood up. There was rapid gunfire from the other side. One bullet brushed past his left arm. He fell to the ground. Some enemy soldiers, taking advantage of this confusion, began to run across open ground to securer positions. Rab Nawaz ordered his platoon to attack the hill. Three were killed, but the others managed to capture the position with Rab Nawaz in the lead.

He found Ram Singh lying on the bare ground. He had been shot in the stomach. His eyes lit up when he saw Rab Nawaz. 'You potter's ass, whatever did you do that for?' he asked.

Rab Nawaz felt as if it was he who had been shot. But he smiled, bent over Ram Singh and began to undo his belt. 'Pig's trotters, who told you to stand up?'

'I was only trying to show myself to you, but you shot me,' Ram Singh said with difficulty. Rab Nawaz unfastened his belt. It was a very bad wound and bleeding profusely.

Rab Nawaz's voice choked, 'I swear upon God, I only fired out of fun. How could I know it was you? You were always an ass, Ram Singha.'

Ram Singh was rapidly losing blood. Rab Nawaz was surprised he was still alive. He did not want to move him. He spoke to his platoon commander, Major Aslam, on the wireless, requesting urgent medical help.

He was sure it would take a long time to arrive. He had a feeling Ram Singh wouldn't last that long. But he laughed. 'Don't you worry. The doctor is on his way.'

Ram Singh said in a weak voice, 'I am not worried, but tell me, how many of my men did you kill?'

'Just one,' Rab Nawaz said.

'And how many did you lose?'

'Six,' Rab Nawaz lied.

'Six,' Ram Singh said. 'When I fell, they were disheartened, but I told them to fight on, give it everything they'd got. Six, yes.' Then his mind began to wander.

He began to talk of their village, their childhood, stories from school, the 6/9 Jat Regiment, its commanding officers, affairs with strange women in strange cities. He was in excruciating pain, but he carried on. 'Do you remember that madam, you pig?'

'Which one?' Rab Nawaz asked.

'That one in Italy. You remember what we used to call her? Maneater.'

Rab Nawaz remembered her. 'Yes, yes. She was called Madam Minitafanto or some such thing. And she used to say: no money, no action. But she had a soft spot for you, that daughter of Mussolini.'

Ram Singh laughed loudly, causing blood to gush out of his wound. Rab Nawaz dressed it with a makeshift bandage. 'Now keep quiet,' he admonished him gently.

Ram Singh's body was burning. He did not have the strength to speak, but he was talking nineteen to the dozen. At times he would stop, as if to see how much petrol was still left in his tank.

After some time, he went into a sort of delirium. Briefly, he would come out of it, only to sink again. During one brief moment of clarity, he said to Rab Nawaz, 'Tell me truthfully, do you people really want Kashmir?'

'Yes, Ram Singha,' Rab Nawaz said passionately.

'I don't believe that. You have been misled,' Ram Singh said.

'No, you have been misled, I swear by the Holy Prophet and his family,' Rab Nawaz said.

'Don't take that oath . . . you must be right.' But there was a strange look on his face, as if he didn't really believe Rab Nawaz.

A little before sunset, Major Aslam arrived with some soldiers. There was no doctor. Ram Singh was hovering between consciousness and delirium. He was muttering, but his voice was so weak that it was difficult to follow him.

Major Aslam was an old 6/9 Jat Regiment officer. Ram Singh had served under him for years. He bent over the dying soldier and called his name, 'Ram Singh, Ram Singh.'

Ram Singh opened his eyes and stiffened his body as if he was coming to attention. With one great effort, he raised his arm and saluted. A strange look of incomprehension suddenly suffused his face. His arm fell limply to his side and he murmured, 'Ram Singh, you ass, you forgot this was a war, a war . . .' He could not complete the sentence. With half-open eyes, he looked at Rab Nawaz, took one last breath and died.

THE WOMAN IN THE RED RAINCOAT

This dates back to the time when both east and west Punjab were being ravaged by bloody communal riots between Hindus and Muslims. It had been raining hard for many days and the fire that men had been unable to put out had been extinguished by nature. However, there was no let-up in the murderous attacks on the innocent, nor was the honour of young women safe. Gangs of young men were still on the prowl and abductions of helpless and terrified girls were common.

On the face of it, murder, arson and looting are really not as difficult to commit as some people think. However, my friend 'S' had not found the going so easy.

But before I tell you his story, let me introduce 'S'. He's a man of ordinary looks and build and is as interested in getting something for nothing as most of us are. But he isn't cruel by nature. It is another matter that he became the perpetrator of a strange tragedy, though he did not quite realize at the time what was happening.

He was just an ordinary student when we were in school, fond of games, but not very sporting. He was always the first to get into a fight when an argument developed during a game. Although he never quite played fair, he was an honest fighter.

He was interested in painting, but he had to leave college after only one year. Next we knew, he had opened a bicycle shop in the city.

When the riots began, his was one of the first shops to be burnt down. Having nothing else to do, he joined the roaming bands of looters and arsonists, nothing extraordinary at the time. It was really more by way of entertainment and diversion than out of a feeling of communal revenge, I would say. Those were strange times. This is his story and it is in his own words.

'It was really pouring down. It seemed as if the skies would burst. In my entire life, I had never seen such rain. I was at home, sitting on my balcony, smoking a cigarette. In front of me lay a large pile of goods I had looted from various shops and houses with the rest of the gang. However, I was not interested in them. They had burnt down my shop but, believe me, it did not really seem to matter, mainly because I had seen so much looting and destruction that nothing made any sense any longer. The noise of the rain was difficult to ignore but, strangely enough, all I was conscious of was a dry and barren silence. There was a stench in the air. Even my cigarette smelt unpleasant. I'm not sure I was thinking even. I was in a kind of daze. Very difficult to explain. Suddenly a shiver ran down my spine and a powerful desire to run out and pick up a girl took hold of me. The rain had become even heavier. I got up, put on my raincoat and, fortifying myself with a fresh tin of cigarettes from the pile of loot, went out in the rain.

'The roads were dark and deserted. Not even soldiers—a common sight in those days—were around. I kept walking about aimlessly for hours. There were many dead bodies lying on the streets, but they seemed to have no effect on me. After some time, I found myself in the Civil Lines area. The roads were without any sign of life. Suddenly I heard the sound of an approaching car. I turned. It was a small Austin being driven at breakneck speed. I don't know what came over me, but I placed myself in the middle of the road and began to wave frantically for the driver to stop.

'The car did not slow down. However, I was not going to move. When it was only a few yards away, it suddenly swerved to the left. In trying to run after it, I fell down, but got up immediately. I hadn't hurt myself. The car braked, then skidded and went off the road. It finally came to a stop, resting against a tree. I began to move towards it. The door was thrown open and a woman in a red raincoat jumped out. I couldn't see her face, but her shimmering raincoat was visible in the murky light. A wave of heat gripped my body.

'When she saw me moving towards her, she broke into a run.

However, I caught up with her after a few yards. "Help me," she screamed as my arms enveloped her tightly, more her slippery raincoat than her, come to think of it.

'"Are you a Englishwoman?" I asked her in English, realizing too late that I should have said "an", not "a".

'"No," she replied.

'I hated Englishwomen, so I said to her, "Then it's all right."

'She began to scream in Urdu, "You're going to kill me. You're going to kill me."

'I said nothing. I was only trying to guess her age and what she looked like. The hood of her raincoat covered her face. When I tried to remove it, she put both her hands in front of her face. I didn't force her. Instead, I walked towards the car, opened the rear door and pushed her in. I started the car and the engine caught. I put it in reverse and it responded. I steered it carefully back on to the road and took off.

'I switched off the engine when we were in front of my house. My first thought was to take her to the balcony, but I changed my mind, not being sure if she would willingly walk up all those stairs. I shouted for the houseboy. "Open the living room door," I told him. After he had done that, I pushed her into the room. In the dark, I caught hold of her and gently pushed her on to the sofa.

'"Don't kill me. Don't kill me please," she began to scream.

'It sounded funny. In a mock-heroic voice I said, "I won't kill you. I won't kill you, darling."

'She began to cry. I sent the servant, who was still hanging around, out of the house. I pulled out a box of matches from my pocket, but the rain had made it damp. There hadn't been any power for weeks. I had a torch upstairs but I didn't really want to bother. "I'm not exactly going to take pictures that I should need a light," I said to myself. I took off my raincoat and threw it on the floor. "Let me take yours," I suggested to her.

'I fumbled for her on the sofa but she wasn't there. However, I wasn't worried. She had to be in the room somewhere. Methodically, I began to comb the place and in a few minutes I found her. In fact, we had a near collision on the floor. I touched her on the throat by accident. She screamed. "Stop that," I said. "I'm not going to kill you."

'I ignored her sobbing and began to unbutton her raincoat, which was made of some plastic material and was very slippery. She kept wailing and trying to struggle free, but I managed to get her free of that silly coat of hers. I realized that she was wearing a sari underneath. I touched her knee and it felt solid. A violent electric current went through my entire body. But I didn't want to rush things.

'I tried to calm her down. "Darling, I didn't bring you here to murder you. Don't be afraid. You are safer here than you would be outside. If you want to leave, you are free to do so. However, I would suggest that as long as these riots last, you should stay here with me. You're an educated girl. Out there, people have become like wild beasts. I don't want you to fall into the hands of those savages."

'"You won't kill me?" she sobbed.

'"No sir," I said.

'She burst out laughing because I had called her sir. However, her laughter encouraged me. "Darling, my English is rather weak," I said with a laugh.

'She did not speak for some time. Then she said, "If you don't want to kill me, why have you brought me here?"

'It was an awkward question. I couldn't think of an answer, but I heard myself saying, "Of course I don't want to kill you for the simple reason that I don't like killing people. So why have I brought you here? Well, I suppose because I'm lonely."

'"But you have your live-in servant."

'"He is only a servant. He doesn't matter."

'She fell silent. I began to experience a sense of guilt, so I got up and said, "Let's forget about it. If you want to leave, I won't stop you."

'I caught hold of her hand, then I thought of her knee which I had touched. Violently, I pressed her against my chest. I could feel her warm breath under my chin. I put my lips on hers. She began to tremble. "Don't be afraid, darling. I won't kill you," I whispered.

'"Please let me go," she said in a tremulous voice.

'I gently pulled my arms away, but then on an impulse I lifted her off the ground. The flesh on her hips was extremely soft, I noticed. I also found that she was carrying a small handbag. I laid her down on the sofa and took her bag away. "Believe me, if it contains valuables, they will be quite safe. In fact, if you like, there are things I can give you," I told her by way of reassurance.

'"I don't need anything," she said.

'"But there is something I need," I replied.

'"What?" she asked.

'"You," I answered.

'She didn't say anything. I began to rub her knee. She offered no resistance. Feeling that she might think I was taking advantage of her helplessness, I said, "I don't want to force you. If you don't want it, you can leave, really."

'I was about to get up, when she grabbed my hand and put it on her breast. Her heart was beating violently. I became excited. "Darling," I whispered, taking her into my arms again.

'We began to kiss each other with reckless abandon. She kept cooing "darling" and God knows what nonsense I myself spoke during that mad interlude.

'"You should take those things off," I suggested.

'"Why don't you take them off yourself?" she answered in an emotional voice.

'I began to caress her. "Who are you?" she asked.

'I was in no mood to tell her, so I said, "I am yours, darling."

'"You're a naughty boy," she said coquettishly, while pressing me close to her. I was now trying to take off her blouse, but she said to me, "Please don't make me naked."

'"What does it matter? It's dark," I said.

'"No, no!"

'She lifted my hands and began to kiss them. "No, please no. I just feel shy."

'"Forget about the blouse," I said. "It's all going to be fine."

'There was a silence, which she broke. "You're not annoyed, are you?"

'"No, why should I be? You don't want to take off your blouse, so that's fine, but . . ." I couldn't complete the sentence, but then with some effort, I said, "But anyway something should happen. I mean, take off your sari."

'"I am afraid." Her throat seemed to have gone dry.

'"Who are you afraid of?" I asked flirtatiously.

'"I am afraid," she replied and began to weep.

'"There is nothing to be afraid of," I said in a consoling voice. '"I won't hurt you, but if you are really afraid, then let's forget about it. You stay here for a few days and, when you begin to feel at home and are not afraid of me any longer, then we'll see."

'"No, no," she said, putting her head on my thighs. I began to comb her hair with my fingers. After some time, she calmed down, then suddenly she pulled me to her with such force that I was taken aback. She was also trembling violently.

'There was a knock at the door and streaks of light began to filter into the dark room from outside.

'It was the servant. "I have brought a lantern. Would you please take it?"

'"All right," I answered.

'"No, no," she said in a terrified, muffled voice.

'"Look, what's the harm? I will lower the wick and place it in a corner," I said.

'I went to the door, brought the lantern in and placed it in a corner of the room. Since my eyes were not yet accustomed to the light, for a few seconds I could see nothing. Meanwhile, she had moved into the farthest corner.

'"Come on now," I said, "we can sit in the light and chat for a few minutes. Whenever you wish, I will put the lantern out."

'Picking up the lantern, I took a few steps towards her. She had covered her face with her sari. "You're a strange girl," I said, "after all, I'm like your bridegroom."

'Suddenly there was a loud explosion outside. She rushed forward and fell into my arms. "It's only a bomb," I said. "Don't be afraid. It's nothing these days."

'"My eyes were now beginning to get used to the light. Her face began to come into focus. I had a feeling that I had seen it before, but I still couldn't see it clearly.

'I put my hands on her shoulders and pulled her closer. God, I can't explain to you what I saw. It was the face of an old woman, deeply painted and yet lined with creases. Because of the rain, her make-up had become patchy. Her hair was coloured, but you could see the roots, which were white. She had a band of plastic flowers across her forehead. I stared at her in a state bordering on shock. Then I put the lantern down and said, "You may leave if you wish."

'She wanted to say something, but when she saw me picking up her raincoat and handbag, she decided not to. Without looking at her, I handed her things to her. She stood for a few minutes staring at her feet, then opened the door and walked out.'

After my friend had finished his story, I asked him, 'Did you know who that woman was?'

'No,' he answered.

'She was the famous artist Miss "M",' I told him.

'Miss "M",' he screamed, 'the woman whose paintings I used to try to copy at school?'

'Yes. She was the principal of the art college and she used to teach her women students still-life painting. She hated men.'

'Where is she now?' he asked suddenly.

'In heaven,' I replied.

'What do you mean?' he asked.

'That night when you let her out of your house, she died in a car accident. You are her murderer. In fact, you are the murderer of two women. One, who is known as a great artist, and the other who was born from the body of the first woman in your living room that night and whom you alone know.'

My friend said nothing.

THE PRICE OF FREEDOM

The year I do not remember, but there was great revolutionary fervour in Amritsar. 'Inqilab Zindabad'—long live revolution—was the slogan of the day. There was excitement in the air and a feeling of restlessness and youthful abandon. We were living through heady times. Even the fearful memories of the Jallianwala Bagh massacre had disappeared, at least on the surface. One felt intensely alive and on the threshold of something great and final.

People marched through the streets every day raising slogans against the Raj. Hundreds were arrested for breaking the law. In fact, courting arrest had become something of a popular diversion. You were picked up in the morning and quite often released by the evening. A case would be registered, a hearing held and a short sentence awarded. You came out, raised a few more slogans and were put in gaol again.

There was so much to live for in those days. The slightest incident sometimes led to the most violent upheaval. One man would stand on a podium in one of the city squares and call for a strike. A strike would follow. There was of course the movement to wear only Indian-spun cotton with the object of putting the Lancashire textile mills out of business. There was a boycott of all imported cloth in effect. Every street had its own bonfire. People would walk up, take off every imported piece of clothing they were wearing and chuck it into the fire. Sometimes a woman would stand on her balcony and throw down her imported silk sari into the bonfire. The crowd would cheer.

I remember this huge bonfire the boys had lit in front of the town hall and the police headquarters, where in a wild moment my classmate Sheikhoo had taken off his silk jacket and thrown it into the flames. A big cheer had gone up because it was well known that he was the son of one of the richest men of the city, who also had the dubious distinction of being the most infamous 'toady', as government sympathizers were popularly called. Inspired by the applause, Sheikhoo had also taken off his silk shirt and sent it the way of his jacket. It was only later that he remembered the gold cufflinks that had gone with it.

I don't want to make fun of my friend, because in those days I too was in the same turbulent frame of mind. I used to dream about getting hold of guns and setting up a secret terrorist organization. That my father was a government servant did not bother me. I was restless and did not even understand what I was restless about.

I was never much interested in school, but during those days I had completely gone off my books. I would spend the entire day at Jallianwala Bagh. Sitting under a tree, I would watch the windows of the houses bordering the park and dream about the girls who lived behind them. I was sure one of these days one of them would fall in love with me.

Jallianwala Bagh had become the hub of the movement of civil disobedience launched by the Congress. There were small and big tents and colourful awnings everywhere. The largest tent was the political headquarters of the city. Once or twice a week, a 'dictator'—for that was what he was called—would be nominated by the people to 'lead the struggle'. He would be ceremoniously placed in the large tent; volunteers would provide him with a ragtag guard of honour, and for the next few days he would receive delegations of young political workers, all wearing homespun cotton. It was also the 'dictator's' duty to get donations of food and money from the city's big shopkeepers and businessmen. And so it would continue until one day the police came and picked him up.

I had a friend called Ghulam Ali. Our intimacy can be judged by the fact that both of us had failed our school leaving examination twice in a row. Once, we had run away from home and were on our way to Bombay—from where we planned to sail for the Soviet Union—when our money ran out. After sleeping for a few nights on footpaths, we had written to our parents and promised not to do such a thing again. We were reprieved.

Shahzada Ghulam Ali, as he later came to be called, was a handsome young man, tall and fair as Kashmiris tend to be. He always walked with a certain swagger that one generally associates with 'tough guys'. Actually, he was no Shahzada—which means prince—when we were at school. However, after having become active in the civil disobedience movement and run the gamut of revolutionary speeches, public processions, social intercourse with pretty female volunteer workers, garlands, slogans and patriotic songs, he had for some reason come to be known as Shahzada.

His fame spread like wildfire in the city of Amritsar. It was a small place where it did not take you long to become famous or infamous. The natives of Amritsar, though by nature critical of the general run of humanity, were rather indulgent when it came to religious and political leaders. They always seemed to have this peculiar need for fiery sermons and revolutionary speeches. Leaders had always had a long tenure in our city. The times were advantageous because the established leadership was in gaol and there were quite a few empty chairs waiting to be occupied. The movement needed people like Ghulam Ali who would be seen for a few days in Jallianwala Bagh, make a speech or two and then duly get arrested.

In those days, the German and Italian dictatorships were the new thing in Europe, which is what had perhaps inspired the Indian National Congress to designate certain party workers as 'dictators'. When Shahzada Ghulam Ali's turn came to go to gaol, as many as forty 'dictators' had already been put inside.

When I learnt that Ghulam Ali had been named the current 'dictator', I made my way to Jallianwala Bagh. There were volunteers outside the big tent. However, since Ghulam Ali had seen me, I was permitted to go in. A white cotton carpet had been laid on the ground and there sat Ghulam Ali, propped up against cushions. He was talking to a group of cotton-clad city shopkeepers about the vegetable trade, I think. After having got rid of them he issued a few instructions to his volunteers and turned to me. He looked too serious, which I thought was funny. When we were alone, I asked him, 'And how is our prince?'

I also realized that he had changed. To my attempt at treating the whole thing as a farce, he said, 'No, Saadat, don't make fun of it. The great honour that has been bestowed on me, I do not deserve. But from now on the movement is going to be my life.'

I promised to return in the evening as he told me that he would be making a speech. When I arrived, there was a large crowd of people around a podium they had set up for the occasion. Then I heard loud applause and there was Shahzada Ghulam Ali. He looked very handsome in his spotless white and his swagger seemed to add to his appeal.

He spoke for an hour or so. It was an emotional speech. Even I was overcome. There were moments when I wished for nothing more than to turn into a human bomb and explode for the glory of the freedom of India.

This happened many years ago and memory always plays tricks with detail, but as I write this I can see Ghulam Ali addressing that turbulent crowd. It was not politics I was conscious of while he spoke, but youth and the promise of revolution. He had the sincere recklessness of a young man who might stop a woman on the street and say to her without any preliminaries, 'Look, I love you.'

Such were the times. I think both the British Raj and the people it ruled were still inexperienced and quite unaware of the consequences of their actions. The government, without really fully comprehending the implications, was putting people in gaol by the thousands, and those who were going to gaol were not quite sure what they were doing and what the results would be.

There was much disorder. I think you could liken the general atmosphere to a spreading fire that leaps out into the air and then just as suddenly goes out, only to ignite again. These sudden eruptions that died just as suddenly, only to burst into flame once again, had created much heat and agitation in the lacklustre, melancholy state of slavery.

As Shahzada Ghulam Ali finished speaking, the entire Jallianwala Bagh came to its feet. I stepped forward to congratulate him, but his eyes were elsewhere. My curiosity was soon satisfied. It was a girl in a white cotton sari, standing behind a flowering bush.

The next day I learnt that Shahzada Ghulam Ali was in love with the girl I had seen the previous evening. And so was she with him, and just as much. She was a Muslim, an orphan, who worked as a nurse at the local women's hospital. I think she was the first Muslim girl in Amritsar to join the Congress movement against the Raj.

Her white cotton saris, her association with the Congress and the fact that she worked in a hospital had all combined to soften that slight stiffness one finds in Muslim girls. She was not beautiful, but she was very feminine. She had acquired that hard-to-describe quality so characteristic of Hindu girls—a mixture of humility, self-assurance and the urge to worship. In her, the beauty of ritualistic Muslim prayer and Hindu devotion to temple gods had been alchemized.

She worshipped Shahzada Ghulam Ali and he loved her to distraction. They had met during a protest march and fallen for each other almost immediately.

Ghulam Ali wanted to marry Nigar before his inevitable and almost eagerly awaited arrest. Why he wanted to do that I am unable to say as he could just as well have married her after his release. Gaol terms in those days varied between three months and a year. There were some who were let out after ten or fifteen days in order to make way for fresh entrants.

All that was really needed was the blessing of Babaji.

Babaji was one of the great figures of the time. He was camped at the splendid house of the richest jeweller in the city, Hari Ram. Normally, Babaji used to live in his village ashram, but whenever he came to Amritsar he would stay with Hari Ram, and the palatial residence, located outside the city, would turn into a sort of shrine, since the number of Babaji's followers was legion. You could see them standing in line, waiting to be admitted briefly to the great man's presence for what was called darshan, or a mere look at him. The old man would receive them sitting cross-legged on a specially constructed platform in a grove of mango trees, accepting donations and gifts for his ashram. In the evening, he would have young women volunteers sing him Hindu devotional songs.

Babaji was known for his piety and scholarship, and his followers included men and women of every faith—Hindus, Muslims, Sikhs and untouchables.

Although on the face of it Babaji had nothing to do with politics, it was an open secret that no political movement in the Punjab could begin or end without his clearance. To the government machinery, he was an unsolved puzzle. There was always a smile on his face, which could be interpreted in a thousand ways.

The civil disobedience movement in Amritsar, with its daily arrests and processions, was quite clearly being conducted with Babaji's blessing, if not his direct guidance. He was in the habit of dropping hints about the tactics to be followed and the next day every major political leader in the Punjab would be wearing Babaji's wisdom as a kind of amulet around his neck.

There was a magnetic quality about him and his voice was soft, persuasive and full of nuances. Not even the most trenchant criticism could ruffle his composure. To his enemies he was an enigma because he always kept them guessing.

Babaji was a frequent visitor to Amritsar, but somehow I had never seen him. Therefore, when Ghulam Ali told me one day that he planned to call on the great man to obtain his blessing for his intended marriage to Nigar, I asked him to take me along. The next day, Ghulam Ali arranged for a tonga, and the three of us—Ghulam Ali, Nigar and I—found ourselves at Hari Ram's magnificent house.

Babaji had already had his ritualistic morning bath—ashnan—and his devotions were done. He now sat in the mango grove listening to a stirring patriotic song, courtesy of a young, beautiful Kashmiri Pandit girl. He sat cross-legged on a mat made from date-palm leaves, and though there were plenty of cushions around, he did not seem to want any. He was in his seventies but his skin was without blemish. I wondered if it was the result of his famous olive oil massage every morning.

He smiled at Ghulam Ali and asked us to join him on the

floor. It was obvious to me that Ghulam Ali and Nigar were less interested in the revolutionary refrain of the song, which seemed to have Babaji in a kind of trance, than their own symphony of young love. At last the girl finished, winning in the bargain Babaji's affectionate approval, indicated with a subtle nod of his head, and he turned to us.

Ghulam Ali was about to introduce Nigar and himself, but he never got an opportunity, thanks to Babaji's exceptional memory for names and faces. In his low, soothing voice he inquired, 'Prince, so you have not yet been arrested?'

'No sir,' Ghulam Ali replied, his hands folded as a mark of respect.

Playing with a pencil, which he had pulled out from somewhere, Babaji said, 'But I think you have already been arrested.' He looked meaningfully at Nigar. 'She has already arrested our prince.'

Babaji's next remark was addressed to the girl who had earlier been singing. 'These children have come to seek my blessing. Tell me, when are you going to get married, Kamal?'

Her pink face turned even pinker. 'But how can I? I am already at the ashram.'

Babaji sighed, turned to Ghulam Ali and said, 'So you two have made up your minds.'

'Yes,' they answered together. Babaji smiled.

'Decisions can sometimes be changed,' he said.

And despite the reverence-laden atmosphere, Ghulam Ali answered, 'This decision can be put off, but it can never be changed.'

Babaji closed his eyes and asked in a lawyer's voice, 'Why?'

Ghulam Ali did not hesitate. 'Because we are committed to it as we are committed to the freedom of India, and while circumstances may change the timing of that event, it is final and immutable.'

Babaji smiled. 'Nigar,' he said, 'why don't you join our ashram because Shahzada is going to gaol in a few days anyway?'

'I will,' she whispered.

Babaji changed the subject and began to ask us about political activities in Jallianwala Bagh. For the next hour or so, the conversation revolved around arrests, processions and even the price of vegetables. I did not join in these pleasantries, but I did wonder why Babaji had been so reluctant to accord his blessing to the young couple. Was he not quite sure that they were in love? Why had he asked Nigar to join the ashram? Was it to help her not to think of Ghulam Ali being in gaol, or did it mean that if she joined the ashram she would not be allowed to marry?

And what was going to happen to Nigar once she was admitted to the rarefied surroundings of the ashram? Would she spend her time intoning devotional and patriotic songs for the spiritual and political enlightenment of Babaji? Would she be happy? I had seen many ashram inmates in my time. There was something lifeless and pallid about them, despite their early morning cold baths and long walks. With their pale faces and sunken eyes, they somehow always reminded me of cows' udders. I couldn't see Nigar living among them, she who was so young and fresh, made up entirely, it seemed to me, of honey, milk and saffron. What had ashrams got to do with India's freedom?

I had always hated ashrams, seminaries, saints' shrines and orphanages. There was something unnatural about these places. I had often seen young boys walking in single file on the street, led by men who administered these institutions. I had visited religious seminaries and schools with their pious inmates. The older ones always wore long beards and the adolescents walked around with sparse, ugly hair sprouting out of their chins. Despite their five prayers a day, their faces never showed any trace of that inner light prayer is supposed to bring about.

Nigar was a woman, not a Muslim, Hindu, Sikh or Christian, but a woman. I simply could not see her praying like a machine every morning at the ashram. Why should she, who was herself pure as a prayer, raise her hands to heaven?

When we were about to leave, Babaji told Ghulam Ali and Nigar that they had his blessing and he would perform the marriage the next day in (where else?) Jallianwala Bagh. He arrived as promised. He was accompanied by his usual entourage of volunteers, with Hari Ram the jeweller in tow. A much-bedecked podium had been put up for the ceremony. The girls had taken charge of Nigar and she made a lovely bride. Ghulam Ali had made no special arrangements. All day long, he had been doing his usual chores, raising donations for the movement and the like. Both of them had decided to hoist the Congress flag after it was all over.

Just before Babaji's arrival, I had been telling Ghulam Ali that we must never forget what had happened in Jallianwala Bagh a few years earlier, in 1919 to be exact. There was a well in the park, which people say was full of dead bodies after General Dyer had ordered his soldiers to stop firing at the crowd. Today, I had told him, the well was used for drinking water, which was still sweet. It bore no trace of the blood that had been spilt so wantonly by the British general and his Gurkha soldiers. The flowers still bloomed and were just as beautiful as they had been on that day.

I had pointed out to Ghulam Ali a house that overlooked the park. It was said that a young girl, who was standing at her window watching the massacre, had been shot through the heart. Her blood had left a mark on the wall below. If you looked carefully, you could still perhaps see it. I remember that six months after the massacre, our teacher had taken the entire class to Jallianwala Bagh and, picking up a piece of earth from the ground, had said to us, 'Children, never forget that the blood of our martyrs is part of this earth.'

Babaji was given a military-style salute by the volunteers. He and Ghulam Ali were taken around the camp, and as the evening was falling the girls began to sing a devotional song and Babaji sat there listening to it with his eyes closed.

The song ended, and Babaji opened his eyes and said, 'Children, I am here to join these two freedom lovers in holy wedlock.' A cheer went up from the crowd. Nigar was in a sari, which bore the three colours of the flag of the Indian National Congress—saffron, green and white. The ceremony was a combination of Hindu and Muslim rituals.

Then Babaji stood up and began to speak. 'These two children will now be able to serve the nation with even greater enthusiasm.

The true purpose of marriage is comradeship. What is being sanctified today will serve the cause of India's freedom. A true marriage should be free of lust and those who are able to exorcize this evil from their lives deserve our respect.'

Babaji spoke for a long time about his concept of marriage. According to him, the true bliss of marriage could only be experienced if the relationship between man and wife was something more than the physical enjoyment of each other's bodies. He did not think the sexual link was as important as it was made out to be. It was like eating. There were those who ate out of indulgence and there were those who ate to stay alive. The sanctity of marriage was more important than the gratification of the sexual instinct.

Ghulam Ali was listening to Babaji's rambling speech as if in a trance. He whispered something to Nigar as soon as Babaji had finished. Then, standing up on the podium, he said in a voice trembling with emotion, 'I have a declaration to make. As long as India does not win freedom, Nigar and I will live not as husband and wife but as friends.' He looked at his wife. 'Nigar, would you like to mother a child who would be a slave at the moment of his birth? No, you wouldn't.'

Ghulam Ali then began to ramble, going from subject to subject, but basically confining his emotional remarks to the freedom of India from the British Raj. At one point, he looked at Nigar and stopped speaking. To me he looked like a drunken man who realizes too late that he has no money left in his wallet. But he recovered his composure and said to Babaji, 'Both of us need your blessing. You have our solemn word of honour that the vow made today shall be kept.'

The next morning Ghulam Ali was taken in because he had threatened to overthrow the Raj and had declared publicly that he would father no children as long as India was ruled by a foreign power. He was given eight months and sent to the distant Multan gaol. He was Amritsar's fortieth 'dictator' to be gaoled and the forty thousandth prisoner of the civil disobedience movement against the Raj.

At that time most of us were convinced that the ousting of

the British from India was a matter of days. However, the Raj was cleverer than we were prepared to give it credit for. It let the movement come to a boil, then made a deal with the leaders, and everything simmered down.

When the workers began to come out of gaol, they realized that the atmosphere had changed. Wisely, most of them decided to resume their normal, humdrum lives. Shahzada Ghulam Ali was let out after seven months, and while it is true the old popular enthusiasm had gone, he was received by a large crowd at the Amritsar railway station from where he was taken out in a procession through the city. A number of public meetings were also held in his honour, but it was evident that the fire and passion had died out. There was a sense of fatigue among the people. It was as if they were runners in a marathon who had been told by the organizers to stop running, return to the starting point, and begin again.

Years went by, but that heady feeling never returned. In my own life, a number of small and big revolutions came and went. I joined college, but failed my exams twice. My father died and I had to run from pillar to post looking for a job. I finally found a translator's position with a third-class newspaper, but I soon became restless and left. For a time, I joined the Aligarh Muslim University, but fell ill and was sent to the more salubrious climate of Kashmir to recover. After three months there, I moved to Bombay. Disgusted with its frequent Hindu–Muslim riots, I made my way to Delhi, but found it too slow and dull and returned to Bombay, despite its impersonal inhabitants who seemed to have no time for strangers.

It was now eight years since I had left Amritsar. I had no idea what had happened to my old friend or to the streets and squares of my early youth. I had never written to anyone and the fact was that I was not interested in the past or the future. I was living in the present. The past, it seemed to me, was like a sum of money you had already spent, and to think about it was like drawing up a ledger account of money you no longer had.

One afternoon—I had both time and some money—I decided to go looking for a pair of shoes. Once, while passing by the

Army & Navy Store, I had noticed a small shop, which had a very attractive display window. I didn't find that shop, but I noticed another, which looked quite reasonable.

'Show me a pair of shoes with rubber soles,' I told the shop assistant.

'We don't stock them,' he replied.

Since the monsoons were expected any time, I asked him if he could sell me rubber ankle-boots.

'We don't stock those either,' he said. 'Why don't you try the store at the corner? We don't carry rubber or part-rubber footwear at all.'

'Why?' I asked, surprised.

'It's the boss's orders,' he answered.

As I stepped out of this strange place which did not sell rubber shoes, I saw a man carrying a small child. He was trying to buy oranges from a vendor.

'Ghulam Ali,' I screamed excitedly.

'Saadat,' he shouted, embracing me. The child didn't like it and began to cry. He went into the shop and told the assistant with whom I had just been talking to take the child home.

'It's been years, hasn't it?' he said.

He had changed. He was no longer the cotton-clad revolutionary who used to make fiery speeches in Jallianwala Bagh. He looked like a normal, homely man.

My mind went back to his last speech. 'Nigar, would you like to mother a child who would be a slave at birth?'

'Whose child was that?' I asked.

'Mine. I have another one who is older. How many children do you have?' he answered without hesitation.

What had happened? Had he forgotten the vow he had taken that day? Was politics no longer a part of his life? What had happened to his passion for the freedom of India? Where was that firebrand revolutionary I used to know? What had happened to Nigar? What had induced her to beget slave children? Had Ghulam Ali married a second time?

'Let us talk,' he said. 'We haven't seen each other for ages.'

I didn't know where to begin, but he didn't put me to the test.

'This shop belongs to me. I've been living in Bombay for the last two years. I'm told you are a big-time story writer now. Do you remember the old days? How we ran away from home to come to Bombay? God, how time flies!'

We went into the shop. A customer who wanted a pair of tennis shoes was told that he would have to go to the shop at the corner.

'Why don't you stock them? You know I also came here looking for a pair,' I asked.

Ghulam Ali's face fell. 'Let's say I just don't like those things,' he replied.

'What things?'

'Those horrible rubber things. But I'll tell you why,' he said.

The anxious look, which had clouded his handsome face suddenly, cleared. 'That life was rubbish. Believe me, Saadat, I have forgotten about those days when the demon of politics was in my head. I'm very happy. I have a wife and two children and my business is doing well.'

He took me to a room at the back of the store. The assistant had come back. Then he began to talk. I will let him tell his story.

'You know how my political life began. You also know what sort of person I was. I mean we grew up together and we were no angels. I wasn't a strong person and yet I wanted to accomplish something in my life. I swear upon God that I was prepared then, as I am prepared today, to sacrifice even my life for the freedom of India. However, after much reflection, I've come to the conclusion that both the politics of India and its political leadership are immature. There are sudden storms and then all is quiet. There is no spontaneity.

'Look, man may be good or evil, but he should remain the way God made him. You can be virtuous without having your head shaved, without donning saffron robes or covering yourself with ash. Those who advocate such things forget that these external manifestations of virtue, if that be indeed what they are, will only get lost on those who follow them. Only ritual will survive, what led to the ritual will be overlooked. Look at all the great prophets. Their teachings are no longer remembered, but we still have their legacy of crosses, holy threads and unshaven armpit hair. They tell you to kill your baser self. Well, if everyone went ahead and did it, what sort of a world would it be?

'You have no idea what hell I went through because I decided to violate human nature. I made a pledge that I would not produce children. It was made in a moment of euphoria. As time passed, I began to feel that the most vital part of my being was paralysed. What was more, it was my own doing. There were moments when I felt proud of my great vow, but they passed. As the pores of my consciousness began to open, reality seemed to want to defeat my resolve. When I met Nigar after my release, I felt that she had changed. We lived together for one year and we kept our promise to Babaji. It was hell. We were being consumed by the futility of our married life.

'The world outside had changed too. Spun cotton, tricolour flags and revolutionary slogans had lost their power. The tents had disappeared from Jallianwala Bagh. There were only holes in the ground where those grand gatherings used to take place. Politics no longer sent the blood coursing through my veins as it used to.

'I spent most of my time at home and we never spoke our minds to each other. I was afraid of touching her. I did not trust myself. One day, as we sat next to each other, I had a mad urge to take her in my arms and kiss her. I let myself go, but I stopped just in time. It was a tremendous feeling while it lasted. However, in the days that followed, I couldn't get rid of a feeling of guilt.

'There had to be a way out of this absurd situation. One day we hit upon a compromise. We would not produce children. We would take the necessary steps, but we would live like husband and wife.

'Thus began a new chapter in our lives. It was as if a blind man had been given back the sight of one eye. But our happiness did not last. We wanted our full vision restored. We felt unhappy and it seemed that everything in our lives had turned into rubber. Even my body felt blubbery and unnatural. Nigar's agony was even more evident. She wanted to be a mother and she couldn't be. Whenever a child was born in the neighbourhood, she would shut herself in a room.

'I wasn't so keen on children myself because, come to think of it, one did not really have to have them. There were millions of people in the world who seemed to be able to get by without them. I could well be one of them. However, what I could no longer stand was this clammy sensation in my hands. When I ate, it felt as if I was eating rubber. My hands always felt as if they had been soaped and then left unrinsed.

'I began to hate myself. All my sensations had atrophied except this weird, unreal sense of touch, which made everything feel like rubber. All I needed to do was to peel off my terrible affliction with the help of two fingers and throw it as far as possible. But I didn't have the courage.

'I was like a drowning man who clutches at straws. And one day I found the straw I was looking for. I was reading a religious text and there it was. I almost jumped. It said, "If a man and woman are joined in wedlock, it is obligatory for them to procreate." And that day I peeled off my curse and have never looked back.'

At this moment, a servant entered the room. He was carrying a child who was holding a balloon. There was a bang and all the child was left with was a piece of string with a shrivelled piece of ugly rubber dangling at the other end.

With two fingers, Ghulam Ali carefully picked up the deflated balloon and threw it away as if it were a particularly disgusting piece of filth.

MOZAIL

Tarlochan looked up at the night sky for the first time in four years, and only because he felt tired and listless. That was what had brought him out on the terrace of Advani Chambers to take the open air and think.

The sky was absolutely clear, free of cloud, stretched over the entire city of Bombay like a huge dust-coloured tent. As far as the eye could see, there were lights. Tarlochan felt as if a lot of stars had fallen from the sky and lodged themselves in tall buildings that looked like huge trees in the dark of the night. The lights shimmered like glow-worms.

This was a new experience for Tarlochan, a new feeling, his being under the open night sky. He felt that he had been imprisoned in his flat for four years and thus deprived of one of nature's great blessings. It was close to three and the breeze was light and pleasant after the heavy, mechanically stirred air of the fan under which he always slept. In the morning when he got up, he always felt as if he had been beaten up all night. But in the natural morning breeze, he felt every pore in his body happily sucking in the air's freshness. When he had come up, he was restless and agitated but now, half an hour later, he felt relaxed. He could think clearly.

He began to think of Kirpal Kaur. She and her entire family lived in a mohalla, which was predominantly and ferociously Muslim. Many houses had been set on fire there and several lives had been lost. Tarlochan would have evacuated the entire family except that a curfew had been clamped down—probably a forty-eight-hour one—and Tarlochan was helpless. There were Muslims all around, and pretty bloodthirsty Muslims they were. News was pouring in from the Punjab about atrocities being committed on Muslims by Sikhs. Any hand—easily a Muslim hand—could grab hold of the soft and delicate wrist of Kirpal Kaur and push her into the well of death.

Kirpal Kaur's mother was blind and her father was a cripple. There was a brother, who lived in Deolali, where he took care of the contract he had recently won.

Tarlochan was really annoyed with Kirpal's brother, Naranjan, who read about the riots every day in the newspaper. In fact, a week ago, he had been told of the rapidity and intensity with which the riots were spreading. He was warned in clear words: 'Forget about your business for the time being. We are passing through difficult times. You should stay with your family or, better still, move to my flat. I know there isn't enough space, but these are not normal times. We'll manage somehow.'

Naranjan had merely smiled through his thick moustache. 'Yaar, you are unduly worried. I have seen many such riots here. This is not Amritsar or Lahore: it is Bombay. You have only been here four years; I have lived here for twelve, a full twelve years.'

God knows what Naranjan thought Bombay was. To him it was a city that would recover from the effects of riots by itself, in case they ever were to take place. He behaved as if he had some magic formula, or a fairy-tale castle that could come to no harm. As for Tarlochan, he could see quite clearly in the cool morning air that this mohalla was not safe. He was even mentally prepared to read in the morning papers that Kirpal Kaur and her parents had been killed.

He did not care much for Kirpal Kaur's crippled father or her blind mother. If they were killed and Kirpal survived, it would be good for Tarlochan. If her brother, Naranjan, was killed in Deolali, it would be even better, as the coast would be clear for Tarlochan. Naranjan was not only a hindrance in his way, but a huge, big boulder blocking his path. Whenever his name came up in a conversation with Kirpal Kaur, he would call him Khingar Singh—Punjabi for 'boulder'—instead of Naranjan Singh.

The breeze was blowing gently, imparting a cool, pleasant sensation to Tarlochan's head, shorn of its long hair, which was a mark of his religion. But his heart was full of apprehensions. Kirpal Kaur had newly entered his life. Although she was the sister of the rough and ruddy Khingar Singh, she was soft, delicate and willowy. She had grown up in the village, lived through its summers and winters, but she did not have that hard, tough, masculine quality that is common to average Sikh village girls, who have to do hard, physical work. She had delicate features as if they were still in the making and her breasts were small, still in need of a few more layers of creamy fat. She was fairer than most Sikh village girls are, fair as unblemished white cotton cloth. Her body was smooth like printed linen. She was very shy.

Tarlochan belonged to the same village but he had not lived there very long. After primary school, he had gone to the city to attend high school and never went back. High school done, he began his life at college and, although during those years he went to his village numerous times, he had never even heard of this girl called Kirpal Kaur. But that may have been because he was always in a hurry to get back to the city.

But those college days were long in the past. Between the college campus and the terrace of the Advani Chambers lay ten years, a period full of strange incidents in Tarlochan's life: Burma, Singapore, Hong Kong—and Bombay, where he had now lived for four years. And it was for the first time in those four years that he had seen the sky at night, which was not a bad sight. In its dust-coloured canopy twinkled thousands of clay lamps while a cool breeze blew his way gently.

The building he lived in was called Advani Chambers and, as he stood on the balcony looking at the pre-morning sky, he thought of Mozail, the Jewish girl who had a flat here. There was a time when he was in love with her 'up to his knees', as he liked to say. Never in his thirty-five years had he felt that way about any woman.

He had run into Mozail the very day he had moved into a second-floor flat at Advani Chambers, which a Christian friend of his had helped him rent. His first impression of her was that she was really quite mad. Her brown hair was cut short and looked dishevelled. She wore thick, unevenly laid lipstick that sat on her lips like congealed blood. She wore a loose white dress, cut so low at the neck that you could see three-quarters of her big breasts with their faint blue veins. Her thin arms were covered with a fine down. She seemed to have just stepped out of a hairdresser's after a haircut. Her lips were not as thick as they looked, but it was the liberal quantities of crimson-red lipstick she plastered on them that gave them the appearance of thick beefsteaks.

Tarlochan's flat faced hers, divided by a narrow passage. When he stepped forward to go into his flat, she stepped out of hers in wooden sandals. He heard their clatter and stopped. She looked at him with her big eyes through her dishevelled hair and laughed. This made Tarlochan nervous and he pulled out his key from his pocket and moved towards his door. One of Mozail's wooden sandals slipped from her foot and came skidding across the floor towards him. Before he could recover, he was on the floor and Mozail was over him, pinning him down. Her trussed-up dress revealed two bare, strong legs which had him in a scissors-like grip. He tried to get up and, in so doing, brushed against her entire body as if soaping it. Breathless now, he apologized to her in very proper words. Mozail straightened her dress and smiled. 'These wooden sandals *ek-dum kandam*, just no good.' Then she carefully re-threaded her big toe in her sandal and walked out of the corridor.

Tarlochan was afraid it might not be easy to befriend her, but she became quite close to him before long. She was headstrong and she did not take Tarlochan too seriously. She would make him take her out to dinner, the cinema or Juhu beach, where she would spend the entire day with him, but whenever he tried to go beyond hands and lips she would tell him to lay off. She would do it in such a way that all his resolve would get entangled in his beard and moustache.

Tarlochan had never been in love before. In Lahore, Burma, Singapore, he would pick up girls and pay for the service. It would never have occurred to him that one day he would find himself plunged 'up to the knees' in love with a wild Jewish girl in Bombay. She treated him with strange indifference, although she would dress up and get ready whenever he asked her to go to the movies with him. Often they would hardly have taken their seats when she would start looking around and, if she found someone she knew, she would wave to him and go sit next to him without asking Tarlochan if he minded.

The same thing would happen in restaurants. He would order an elaborate meal and she would abruptly rise in the middle of it to join an old friend who had caught her eye. Tarlochan would get terribly jealous. And when he protested, she would stop meeting him for days on end and, when he insisted, she would pretend that she had a headache or her stomach was upset. Or she would say, 'You are a Sikh. You are incapable of understanding anything subtle.'

'Such as your lovers?' he would taunt her.

She would put her hands on her hips, spread out her legs and say, 'Yes, my lovers, but why does it burn you up?'

'We cannot carry on like this,' Tarlochan would say.

And Mozail would laugh. 'You're not only a real Sikh, you're also an idiot. In any case, who asked you to carry on with me? I have a suggestion. Go back to your Punjab and marry a Sikhni.' In the end Tarlochan would always give in because Mozail had become his weakness and he wanted to be around her all the time. Often she would humiliate him in front of some young 'Kristan' lout she had picked up that day from somewhere. He would get angry, but not for long.

This cat-and-mouse game with Mozail continued for two years, but he was steadfast. One day when she was in one of her high and happy moods, he took her in his arms and asked, 'Mozail, don't you love me?'

Mozail freed herself, sat down in a chair, gazed intently at her dress, then raised her big Jewish eyes, batted her thick eyelashes and said, 'I cannot love a Sikh.'

'You always make fun of me. You make fun of my love,' he said in an angry voice.

She got up, swung her brown head of hair from side to side and said coquettishly, 'If you shave off your beard and let down your long hair which you keep under your turban, I promise you many men will wink at you suggestively, because you are very dishy.'

Tarlochan felt as if his hair was on fire. He dragged Mozail towards him, squeezed her in his arms and put his bearded lips on hers.

She pushed him away. 'Phew!' she said, 'I brushed my teeth this morning. You don't have to bother.'

'Mozail!' Tarlochan screamed.

She paid no attention, but took out her lipstick from the bag she always carried and began to touch up her lips, which looked havoc-stricken after contact with Tarlochan's beard and moustache.

'Let me tell you something,' she said without looking up. 'You have no idea how to use your hirsute assets properly. They would be perfect for brushing dust off my navy-blue skirt.'

She came and sat next to him and began to unpin his beard. It was true he was very good-looking, but being a practising Sikh he had never shaved a single hair off his body and, consequently, he had come to assume a look that was not natural. He respected his religion and its customs and he did not wish to change any of its ritual formalities.

'What are you doing?' he asked Mozail. By now his beard, freed of its shackles, was hanging over his chest in waves.

'You have such soft hair, so I don't think I would use it to brush my navy-blue skirt. Perhaps a nice, soft woven handbag,' she said, smiling flirtatiously.

'I have never made fun of your religion. Why do you always mock mine? It's not fair. But I have suffered these insults silently because I love you. Did you know I love you?'

'I know,' she said, letting go of his beard.

'I want to marry you,' he declared, while trying to repin his beard.

'I know,' she said with a slight shake of her head. 'In fact, I have nearly decided to marry you.'

'You don't say!' Tarlochan nearly jumped.

'I do,' she said.

He forgot his half-folded beard and embraced her passionately. 'When . . . when?'

She pushed him aside. 'When you get rid of your hair.'

'It will be gone tomorrow,' he said without thinking.

She began to do a tap dance around the room. 'You're talking rubbish, Tarloch. I don't think you have the courage.'

'You will see,' he said defiantly.

'So I will,' she said, kissing him on the lips, followed by her usual 'Phew!'

He could hardly sleep that night. It was not a small decision. However, the next day he went out to a barber in the Fort area and had him cut his hair and shave off his beard. While this operation was in progress, he kept his eyes closed. When it was finished, he looked at his new face in the mirror. It looked good. Any girl in Bombay would have found it difficult not to take a long, second look at him.

He did not leave his flat on his first hairless day, but sent word to Mozail that he was not well and would she mind dropping in for a minute. She stopped dead in her tracks when she saw him. 'My darling Tarloch,' she cried and fell into his arms. She ran her hands over his smooth cheeks and combed his short hair with her fingers. She laughed so much that her nose began to run. She had no handkerchief and calmly she lifted her skirt and wiped it. Tarlochan blushed. 'You should wear something underneath.'

'Gives me a funny feeling. That's how it is,' she replied.

'Let's get married tomorrow,' he said.

'Of course,' she replied, rubbing his chin.

They decided to get married in Poona, where Tarlochan had many friends.

Mozail worked as a salesgirl in one of the big department stores in the Fort area. She told Tarlochan to wait for her at a taxi stand in front of the store the next day, but she never turned up. He later learnt that she had gone off with an old lover of hers who had recently bought a new car. They had moved to Deolali and were not expected to return to Bombay 'for some time'.

Tarlochan was shattered, but in a few weeks he had gotten over it.

And it was at this point that he had met Kirpal Kaur and fallen in love with her.

He now realized what a vulgar girl Mozail was and how

totally heartless. He thanked his stars that he hadn't married her.

But there were days when he missed her. He remembered that once he had decided to buy her some gold earrings and had taken her to a jeweller's, but all she wanted was some cheap baubles. That was the way she was.

She used to lie in bed with him for hours and let him kiss and fondle her as much as he wanted, but she would never let him make love to her. 'You're a Sikh,' she would laugh, 'and I hate Sikhs.'

One argument they always had was over her habit of not wearing any underclothes. Once she said to him, 'You're a Sikh and I know that you wear some ridiculous shorts under your trousers because that is the Sikh religious requirement, but I think it's rubbish that religion should be kept tucked under one's trousers.'

Tarlochan looked at the gradually brightening sky.

'The hell with her,' he said loudly and decided not to think about her at all. He was worried about Kirpal Kaur and the danger that loomed over her.

A number of communal incidents had already taken place in the locality. The place was full of orthodox Muslims and, curfew or no curfew, they could easily enter her house and massacre everyone.

Since Mozail had left him, he had decided to grow his hair. His beard had flourished again, but he had come to a compromise. He would not let it grow too long. He knew a barber who could trim it so skilfully that it would not appear trimmed.

The curfew was still in force, but you could walk about in the street, as long as you did not stray too far. He decided to do so. There was a public tap in front of the building. He sat down under it and began to wash his hair and freshen up his face.

Suddenly he heard the sound of wooden sandals on the cobblestones. There were other Jewish women in that building, all of whom for some reason wore the same kind of sandals. He thought it was one of them.

But it was Mozail. She was wearing her usual loose gown under which he could see her breasts dancing. It disturbed him.

He coughed to attract her attention, because he had a feeling she might just pass him by. She came towards him, examined his beard and said, 'What do we have here, a twice-born Sikh?'

She touched his beard. 'Still good enough to brush my navy-blue skirt with, except that I left it in that other place in Deolali.'

Tarlochan said nothing. She pinched his arm. 'Why don't you say something, Sardar sahib?'

He looked at her. She had lost weight. 'Have you been ill?' he asked.

'No.'

'But you look run down.'

'I am dieting. So you are once again a Sikh?' She sat down next to him, squatting on the ground.

'Yes,' he replied.

'Congratulations. Are you in love with some other girl?'

'Yes.'

'Congratulations. Does she live here, I mean, in our building?'

'No.'

'Isn't that awful?'

She pulled at his beard. 'Is this grown on her advice?'

'No.'

'Well, I promise you that if you get this beard of yours shaved off, I'll marry you. I swear.'

'Mozail,' he said, 'I have decided to marry this simple girl from my village. She is a good, observing Sikh, which is why I am growing my hair again.'

Mozail got up, swung herself in a semi-circle on her heel and said, 'If she's a good Sikh, why should she marry you? Doesn't she know that you once broke all the rules and shaved your hair off?'

'No, she doesn't. I started growing a beard the very day you left me—as a gesture of revenge, if you like. I met her some time later, but the way I tie my turban, you can hardly tell that I don't have a full head of hair.'

She lifted her dress to scratch her thigh. 'Damn these mosquitoes,' she said. Then she added, 'When are you getting married?'

'I don't know.' The anxiety in his voice showed.

'What are you thinking, Tarlochan?' she asked. He told her.

'You are a first-class idiot. What's the problem? Just go and get her here where she will be safe.'

'Mozail, you can't understand these things. It's not that simple. You don't really give a damn and that is why we broke up. I'm sorry,' he said.

'Sorry? Come off it, you silly idiot. What you should be thinking of now is how we can get . . . whatever her name is . . . to your flat. And here you go talking about your sorrow at losing me. It could never have worked. Your problem is that you are both stupid and cautious. I like my men to be reckless. OK, forget about that, let's go and get your whatever Kaur from wherever she is.'

Tarlochan looked at her nervously. 'But there's a curfew in the area,' he said.

'There's no curfew for Mozail. Let's go,' she said, almost dragging him.

She looked at him and paused. 'What's the matter?' he asked.

'Your beard, but it's not that long. However, take that turban off, then nobody will take you for a Sikh.'

'I won't go bareheaded,' he said.

'Why not?'

'You don't understand? It is not proper for me to go to their house without my turban.'

'And why not?'

'Why don't you understand? She has never seen me except in a turban. She thinks I am a proper Sikh. I daren't let her think otherwise.'

Mozail rattled her wooden sandals on the floor. 'You are not only a first-class idiot, you are also an ass. It is a question of saving her life, whatever that Kaur of yours is called.'

Tarlochan was not going to give up. 'Mozail, you've no idea how religious she is. Once she sees me bareheaded, she'll start hating me.'

'Your love be damned. Tell me, are all Sikhs as stupid as you? On the one hand, you want to save her life and at the same time you insist on wearing your turban, and perhaps even those funny knickers you are never supposed to be without.'

'I do wear my knickers—as you call them—all the time,' he said.

'Good for you,' she said. 'But think, you're going to go to that awful area full of those bloodthirsty Muslims and their big maulanas. If you go in a turban, I promise you they will take one look at you and run a big, sharp knife across your throat.'

'I don't care, but I must wear my turban. I can risk my life, but not my love.'

'You're an ass,' she said exasperatedly. 'Tell me, if you're bombed off, what use will that Kaur be to you? I swear, you're not only a Sikh, you are an idiot of a Sikh.'

'Don't talk rot,' Tarlochan snapped.

She laughed, then she put her arms around his neck and swung her body slightly. 'Darling,' she said, 'then it will be the way you want it. Go put on your turban. I will be waiting for you in the street.'

'You should put on some clothes,' Tarlochan said.

'I'm fine the way I am,' she replied.

When he joined her, she was standing in the middle of the street. Her legs apart like a man, and smoking. When he came close, she blew the smoke in his face. 'You're the most terrible human being I've ever met in my life,' Tarlochan said. 'You know we Sikhs are not allowed to smoke.'

'Let's go,' she said.

The bazaar was deserted. The curfew seemed to have affected even the usually brisk Bombay breeze. It was hardly noticeable. Some lights were on but their glow was sickly. Normally at this hour the trains would start running and shops begin to open. There was absolutely no sign of life anywhere.

Mozail walked in front of him. The only sound came from the impact of her wooden sandals on the road. He almost asked her to take the stupid things off and go barefoot, but he didn't. She wouldn't have agreed.

Tarlochan felt scared, but Mozail was walking ahead of him nonchalantly, puffing merrily on her cigarette. They came to a square and were challenged by a policeman. 'Where are you going?' Tarlochan fell back, but Mozail moved towards the policeman, gave her head a playful shake and said, 'It's you! Don't you know me? I'm Mozail. I'm going to my sister's in the next street because she's sick. That man there is a doctor.'

While the policeman was still trying to make up his mind, she pulled out a packet of cigarettes from her bag and offered him one. 'Have a smoke,' she said.

The policeman took the cigarette. Mozail helped him light it with hers. He inhaled deeply. Mozail winked at him with her left eye and at Tarlochan with her right and they moved on.

Tarlochan was still very scared. He looked left and right as he walked behind her, expecting to be stabbed at any moment. Suddenly she stopped. 'Tarloch dear, it is not good to be afraid. If you're afraid, then something awful always happens. That's my experience.'

He didn't reply.

They came to the street that led to the mohalla where Kirpal Kaur lived. A shop was being looted. 'Nothing to worry about,' she told him. One of the rioters who was carrying something on his head ran into Tarlochan and the object fell to the ground. The man stared at Tarlochan and he knew he was a Sikh. He slipped his hand under his shirt to pull out his knife.

Mozail pushed him away as if she was drunk. 'Are you mad, trying to kill your own brother? This is the man I'm going to marry.' Then she said to Tarlochan, 'Karim, pick this thing up and help put it back on his head.'

The man gave Mozail a lecherous look and touched her breasts with his elbow. 'Have a good time, sali,' he said.

They kept walking and were soon in Kirpal Kaur's mohalla. 'Which street?' she asked.

'The third on the left. That building on the corner,' he whispered.

When they came to the building, they saw a man run out of it and into another across the street. After a few minutes, three men emerged from that building, and rushed into the one where Kirpal Kaur lived. Mozail stopped. 'Tarloch dear, take off your turban,' she said.

'That I'll never do,' he replied.

'Just as you please, but I hope you do notice what's going on.'

Something terrible was going on. The three men had re-emerged, carrying gunny bags with blood dripping from them. Mozail had an idea. 'Look, I'm going to run across the street and go into that building. You should pretend that you're trying to catch me. But don't think. Just do it.'

Without waiting for his response, she rushed across the street and ran into Kirpal Kaur's building, with Tarlochan in hot pursuit. He was panting when he found her in the front courtyard.

'Which floor?' she asked.

'Second.'

'Let's go.' And she began to climb the stairs, her wooden sandals clattering on each step. There were large bloodstains everywhere.

They came to the second floor, walked down a narrow corridor and Tarlochan stopped in front of a door. He knocked. Then he called in a low voice, 'Mehnga Singhji, Mehnga Singhji.'

A girl's voice answered, 'Who is it?'

'Tarlochan.'

The door opened slightly. Tarlochan asked Mozail to follow him in. Mozail saw a very young and very pretty girl standing behind the door trembling. She also seemed to have a cold. Mozail said to her, 'Don't be afraid. Tarlochan has come to take you away.'

Tarlochan said, 'Ask Sardar sahib to get ready, but quickly.'

There was a shriek from the flat upstairs. 'They must have got him,' Kirpal Kaur said, her voice hoarse with terror.

'Whom?' Tarlochan asked.

Kirpal Kaur was about to say something, when Mozail pushed her in a corner and said, 'Just as well they got him. Now take off your clothes.'

Kirpal Kaur was taken aback, but Mozail gave her no time to think. In one moment, she divested her of her loose shirt. The young girl frantically put her arms in front of her breasts. She was terrified. Tarlochan turned his face. Then Mozail took off the kaftan-like gown she always wore and asked Kirpal Kaur to put it on. She was now stark naked herself.

'Take her away,' she told Tarlochan. She untied the girl's hair so that it hung over her shoulders. 'Go.'

Tarlochan pushed the girl towards the door, then turned back. Mozail stood there, shivering slightly because of the cold.

'Why don't you go?' she asked.

'What about her parents?' he said.

'They can go to hell. You take her.'

'And you?'

'Don't worry about me.'

They heard men running down the stairs. Soon they were banging at the door with their fists. Kirpal Kaur's parents were moaning in the other room. 'There's only one thing to do now. I'm going to open the door,' Mozail said.

She addressed Tarlochan, 'When I open the door, I'll rush out and run upstairs. You follow me. These men will be so flabbergasted that they will forget everything and come after us.'

'And then?' Tarlochan asked.

'Then, this one here, whatever her name is, can slip out. The way she's dressed, she'll be safe. They'll take her for a Jew.'

Mozail threw the door open and rushed out. The men had no time to react. Involuntarily, they made way for her. Tarlochan ran after her. She was storming up the stairs in her wooden sandals with Tarlochan behind her.

She slipped and came crashing down, head first. Tarlochan stopped and turned. Blood was pouring out of her mouth and nose and ears. The men who were trying to break into the flat had also gathered round her in a circle, forgetting temporarily what they were there for. They were staring at her naked, bruised body.

Tarlochan bent over her. 'Mozail, Mozail.'

She opened her eyes and smiled. Tarlochan undid his turban and covered her with it.

'This is my lover. He's a bloody Muslim, but he's so crazy that I always call him a Sikh,' she said to the men.

More blood poured out of her mouth. 'Damn it!' she said.

Then she looked at Tarlochan and pushed aside the turban with which he had tried to cover her nakedness.

'Take away this rag of your religion. I don't need it.'

Her arm fell limply on her bare breasts and she said no more.

THE DUTIFUL DAUGHTER

The country had been divided. Hundreds of thousands of Muslims and Hindus were moving from India to Pakistan and from Pakistan to India in search of refuge. Camps had been set up to give them temporary shelter, but they were so overcrowded that it seemed quite impossible to push another human being into them, and yet more refugees were being brought in every day. There wasn't enough food to go round and basic facilities were almost non-existent. Epidemics and infections were common, but it didn't bother anybody. Such were the times.

The year 1948 had begun. Hundreds of volunteers had been assigned the task of recovering abducted women and children and restoring them to their families. They would go in groups to India from Pakistan and from Pakistan to India to make their recoveries.

It always amused me to see that such enthusiastic efforts were being made to undo the effects of something that had been perpetrated by more or less the same people. Why were they trying to rehabilitate the women who had been raped and taken away when they had let them be raped and taken away in the first place?

It was all very confusing, but one still admired the devotion of these volunteers.

It was not a simple task. The difficulties were enormous. The abductors were not easy to trace. To avoid discovery, they had devised various means of eluding their pursuers. They were constantly on the move, from this locality to that, from one city to another. One followed a tip and often found nothing at the end of the trail.

One heard strange stories. One liaison officer told me that in Saharanpur, two abducted Muslim girls had refused to return to their parents who were in Pakistan. Then there was this Muslim girl in Jullandar who was given a touching farewell by the abductor's family as if she was a daughter-in-law leaving on a long journey. Some girls had committed suicide on the way, afraid of facing their parents. Some had lost their mental balance as a result of their traumatic experiences. Others had become alcoholics and retorted with abusive and vulgar language when spoken to.

When I thought about these abducted girls, I only saw their protruding bellies. What was going to happen to them and what they contained? Who would claim the end result? Pakistan or India?

And who would pay the women the wages for carrying those children in their wombs for nine months? Pakistan or India? Or would it all be put down in God's great ledger, that is, if there were still any pages left?

Why were they being described as 'abducted women'? I had always thought that when a woman ran away from home with her lover—the police always called it 'abduction'—it was the most romantic act in the world. But these women had been taken against their will and violated.

They were strange, illogical times. I had boarded up all the doors and windows of my mind, shuttered them up. It was difficult to think straight.

Sometimes it seemed to me that the entire operation was being conducted like import-export trade.

One liaison officer asked me, 'Why do you look lost?'

I didn't answer his question.

Then he told me a story.

'We were looking for abducted women from town to town, village to village, street to street, and sometimes days would go by before we would have any success.

'And almost every time I went across to what is now India, I would notice an old woman, the same old woman. The first time it was in the suburbs of Jullandar. She looked distracted, almost unaware of her surroundings. Her eyes had a desolate look, her clothes had turned to rags and her hair was coated with dust. The only thing that struck me about her was that she was looking for someone.

'I was told by one of the women volunteers that she had lost her mind because her only daughter had been abducted during the riots in Patiala. She said they had tried for months to find the girl but had failed. In all probability, she had been killed, but that was something the old woman was not prepared to believe.

'The next time I ran into her at Saharanpur. She was at the bus stop and she looked much worse than she had the first time I had seen her. Her lips were cracked and her hair looked matted. I spoke to her. I said she should abandon her futile search; and to induce her to follow my advice, I told her—it was brutal—that her daughter had probably been murdered.

'She looked at me. "Murdered? No. No one can murder my daughter. No one can murder my daughter."

'And she walked away.

'It set me thinking. Why was this crazy woman so confident that no one would murder her daughter, that no sharp, deadly knife could slash her throat? Did she think her daughter was immortal or was it her motherhood that would not admit defeat nor entertain the possibility of death?

'On my third visit, I saw her again in another town. She looked very old and ragged. Her clothes were now so threadbare that they hardly covered her frail body. I gave her a change of dress, but she didn't want it. I said to her, "Old woman, I swear to you that your daughter was killed in Patiala."

'"You are lying," she said. There was steely conviction in her voice.

'To convince her, I said, "I assure you I'm telling the truth. You've suffered enough. It's time to go to Pakistan. I'll take you."

'She paid no attention to what I had said and began muttering to herself. "No one can murder my daughter," she suddenly declared in a strong, confident voice.

'"Why?" I asked.

'"Because she's beautiful. She's so beautiful that no one can kill her. No one can even dream of hurting her," she said in a low whisper.

'I wondered if her daughter was really as beautiful as that. I thought it was just a matter of all children being beautiful to their mother. But it was also possible that the old woman was right. Who knew? But in this holocaust nothing had survived. This mad old woman was deceiving herself. There are so many ways of escape from unpleasant reality. Grief is like a roundabout, which one intersects with an infinite number of roads.

'I made many other trips across the border to India and almost every time I somehow ran into the old woman. She was no more than a bag of bones now. She could hardly see and tottered about like a blind person, a step at a time. Only one thing hadn't changed—her faith that her daughter was alive and that no one could kill her.

'One of the women volunteers said to me, "Don't waste your time over her. She's raving mad. It would be good if you could take her to Pakistan with you and put her in an asylum."

'Suddenly, I didn't want to do that. I didn't want to divest her of her only reason for living. As it was, she was in a vast asylum where nothing made any sense. I didn't wish to confine her within the four walls of a regular one.

'The last time I met her was in Amritsar. She looked so broken that it almost brought tears to my eyes. I decided that I would make one last effort to take her to Pakistan.

'There she stood in Farid Chowk, peering around with her half-blind eyes. I was talking to a shopkeeper about an abducted Muslim girl, who, we had been informed, was being kept in the house of a Hindu moneylender.

'After my exchange with the shopkeeper, I crossed the street, determined to persuade the old woman to come with me to Pakistan.

'I noticed a couple. The woman's face was partly covered by her white chaddar. The man was young and handsome—a Sikh.

'As they went past the old woman, the man suddenly stopped. He even fell back a step or two. Nervously, he caught hold of the woman's hand. I couldn't see her full face, but one glimpse was enough to know that she was beautiful beyond words.

'"Your mother," he said to her.

'The girl looked up, but only for a second. Then, covering her face with her chaddar, she grabbed her companion's arm and said, "Let's get away from here."

'They crossed the road, taking long, brisk steps.

'The old woman shouted, "Bhagbari, Bhagbari."

'I rushed towards her. "What is the matter?" I asked.

'She was trembling. "I have seen her . . . I have seen her."

'"Whom have you seen?" I asked.

'"I have seen my daughter . . . I have seen Bhagbari." Her eyes were like burnt-out lights.

'"Your daughter is dead," I said.

'"You're lying," she screamed.

'"I swear on God your daughter is dead."

'The old woman fell in a heap on the road.'

THREE SIMPLE STATEMENTS

Not far from Congress House and Jinnah Hall in Bombay is a urinal, called mootri by the locals, who also have made a habit of dumping all their rubbish outside this facility. The stink it produces is so revolting that you cannot walk past it without covering your nose with your handkerchief.

He was once constrained to go into this hellhole, his nose protected by a handkerchief, while trying all the time not to breathe. The floor was wet and filthy. The walls were covered with crude representations of human genitalia and in one corner someone had scribbled in charcoal the words: 'ram Pakistan up the you-know-what of the Muslims'.

He felt revolted and stepped out as quickly as he could.

Both Congress House and Jinnah Hall were under the control of the government, but the mootri was free, free to spread its stink far and wide, free to receive the garbage of the local community at its doorstep.

A few days later, he found himself visiting the mootri once again to answer the call of nature. He had his face covered and his breath held in his lungs. There was more filth on the floor than the last time and more murals on the wall depicting the engines of human procreation.

Under the words 'ram Pakistan up the you-know-what of the Muslims' someone had scrawled with a thick pencil: 'ram Akhand Bharat up the you-know-what of the Hindus'. He left hurriedly, feeling as if he had been sprayed with acid.

Some time later, Mahatma Gandhi was granted unconditional release by the British Indian government. Mr Jinnah was defeated in the Punjab. As for Congress House and Jinnah Hall, they were neither defeated nor released. And the mootri, which was only a short distance from these imposing buildings, continued to remain under the occupation of malodorous filth. Only the pile of garbage outside had grown larger.

He went for the third time to the mootri—but not to answer the call of nature.

He covered his nose and held his breath as he entered. The floor was crawling with vermin. No further space was left on the wall to draw more human genitalia.

The words 'ram Pakistan up the you-know-what of the Muslims' and 'ram Akhand Bharat up the you-know-what of the Hindus' had somewhat faded.

When he left, a new line had appeared under the two declarations: 'ram Mother India up the you-know-what of both Muslims and Hindus'.

For a moment these words seemed to dispel the stink of the mootri like a light fragrance dancing in the wind—but only for a moment.

JINNAH SAHIB

'The year was 1937. The Muslim League was young—and so was I. I was at an age when you want to do something . . . anything. I was well built and strong, always ready to take on whatever came my way. I was raring to go. I would have even wanted to fashion a creature with my own hands and then go for him in a no-holds-barred physical fight. Such is youth. You are perpetually restless because you want to do things, hoping they will be big things. You simply cannot sit still.'

This was Mohammad Hanif Azad the film actor, a name familiar to most people. Before the partition of the country, he used to be in the movies in Bombay. He has since lived in Lahore, where, like the rest of his fellow actors, he has been struggling to survive, such being the state of the industry in Pakistan. Someone once told me that he had been Quaid-e-Azam Muhammad Ali Jinnah's chauffeur for many years. I was keen to know if it was true and had sought him out one day. I was to hold many more meetings with him to help him relive the old days. But let Azad speak for himself.

'Like Ghalib had once been young, so was I. I do not know if the great poet ever found himself sucked into a political movement, but I can tell you that I was a committed worker of the All India Muslim League. I was a sincere member of the Ghaziabad Corps, as were many other young people like me. I say sincere because sincerity was all I had.

'I recall clearly when Muhammad Ali Jinnah came to Delhi and was taken out in a procession the like of which had not been seen before. We, the youth of Ghaziabad, had played no small part in making the event a great success. Our corps was led by Anwar Qureshi, a strapping young man, who was later known as the poet of Pakistan. He had written a special poem for the occasion, which we were all singing in chorus as we marched. I do not know if we were offbeat, but singing we were and very lustily too. We couldn't care less if the notes that left our throats were right or wrong. Remember what Ghalib said: "It does not matter how you say it nor if what you say is in or out of rhythm. The important thing is to say it." Our historic procession set out from Delhi's historic Jamia Mosque with sky-renting slogans and wound its way to the Muslim League office through Chandni Chowk, Lal Kunwan, Hauz Qazi and Chowri Bazaar.

'It was during this procession, I think, that Muhammad Ali Jinnah was spontaneously given the title of Quaid-e-Azam—the Great Leader. He was in a phaeton drawn by six horses, and every leading Muslim League leader marched that day with us. There were men on cycles, motorbikes and even camel carts. It was all very disciplined, which seemed to please our leader greatly, since he was a strict believer in discipline.

'My response to that procession was deeply emotional. I was completely overwhelmed. I do not even remember now what exactly I felt when I first set eyes on Jinnah sahib. When I look back and analyse my reaction, I realize that I was so taken with him, even before I had seen him, that if someone had pointed at a man, any man, and said to me, "There goes your Quaid-e-Azam," I would have believed him immediately and felt deliriously happy. That's the way faith is. Pure and without the slightest trace of doubt. As our procession wound its way through the streets of old Delhi, I got a chance to look at Jinnah sahib from many angles. Then suddenly a thought came to my mind. How could my Quaid, my Great Leader, be so gaunt, so weak, so frail!

'Ghalib had once marvelled at his beloved actually coming to visit him. In wonder, the poet had gazed at her and then at the home, which she had graced. I felt more or less the same way. I would look at the Quaid's fragile figure and then at my strong and well-built body and wish that I would either shrink or become like him or have him become like me. I had also prayed that he be safe from those who wished him ill, and it was said there were many such.

'Life moved on, and it so happened that this deep and hidden urge I have always had to do something artistic now began to add to my restlessness. One day, therefore, I decided to travel to Bombay and try my luck in that city. I was always inclined towards drama and acting. So here I was, no longer smitten with the desire to serve the nation so much as to become an actor. What a bundle of contradictions a human being is! When I arrived in Bombay, the Imperial Film Company ruled the roost, but it was next to impossible to get into it. But I persisted and finally managed to get a foot in as an extra on a daily wage of eight annas. That did not stop me from dreaming about becoming a great star of the silver screen. I am gregarious by nature. I may not have a sweet tongue but I am not that bad a talker either. Urdu, my mother tongue—something with which all the great stars of the company were unfamiliar—came to my rescue, ironically in Bombay where it was not spoken and not in Delhi where it was. Since the language of the movies was Urdu or Hindustani, I was always in demand to read and write the lines the actors were required to speak. I would also read their fan mail for them and write the replies. However, this reading and writing did not help me in my ambition. Extra I was and extra I remained.

'It was during those days that I became friends with the personal chauffeur—a man named Buddhan—of the owner of the Imperial Film Company, Seth Ardeshir Irani. The first thing he did for me was to teach me how to drive. This he would do during his spare hours, which were not many. He was always afraid that if the seth found out what he was doing he might be laid off. Because of this constraint, and despite my intelligence and enthusiasm, I did not quite master the art of motor driving. All I could manage was to drive Seth Ardeshir Irani's Buick on the arrow-straight roads of Bombay whenever I had the opportunity. As to what made a car move or what its body parts were, I knew absolutely nothing.

'I was obsessed with acting, but that was in my head. My heart was still filled with the love of the Muslim League and its moving spirit, Quaid-e-Azam Muhammad Ali Jinnah. One talked endlessly of the treatment meted out to the Muslims by the Congress, whether while whiling away time at the Imperial Film Company or loafing around Kennedy Bridge, Bhindi Bazaar, Muhammad Ali Road or the Playhouse. Everyone at Imperial knew that I was an ardent Muslim League supporter and a follower of Quaid-e-Azam Muhammad Ali Jinnah. In those days a Hindu did not become your enemy just because you liked the Quaid-e-Azam. The formal demand for Pakistan had yet to be made. Not everyone at the Imperial Company perhaps knew about the Quaid. Some might have thought when I praised him that I was referring to a movie actor whose fan I was. One day, the most celebrated hero of those days, D. Billimoria, passed on a copy of the *Times of India* to me and said, "Look, here is your Jinnah sahib." I thought it was a picture of his which had appeared that day, but when I found nothing on any of the pages, I asked, "But where is his picture then?" Billimoria, who sported a John Gilbert moustache, smiled and said, "There is no photo-voto but an ad." "What kind of an ad?" I asked. Billimoria took the paper away from me and pointed at a column. "Mr Jinnah wants a motor mechanic who can take charge of his garage and all the cars in it." I looked at the spot that Billimoria had touched with his forefinger and said, "Oh!" as if I had read every word instantaneously, though the fact was that I knew about as much English as Billimoria did Urdu.

'As I have already said, my driving prowess consisted of the ability to get the car moving, provided the road was straight like an arrow. I was quite ignorant about how cars worked. All I knew was that when you pressed the self-starter the engine caught. Sometimes it failed to do so, but if someone had asked me why, I would have replied that it was all part of the immutable laws of motor driving, which the human mind could not fathom. I asked Billimoria what address the ad carried and memorized it. Next morning, I decided to go to the Quaid-e-Azam's house, not to get the job but to get a chance to see him again. The only diploma I had under my arm was my devotion to the Quaid. I arrived at his residence on Mount Pleasant Road, Malabar Hill. There was a Pathan security guard outside the magnificent bungalow, wearing a spotless, generously cut white shalwar and a huge silk turban, tied just right. I was delighted. Here was another well-built man. Mentally, I tried to compare myself with him and was satisfied that the difference, if any, was marginal.

'There were quite a few hopefuls there already, and each of them had certificates and diplomas testifying to his suitability for the position. I joined them quietly. I might add that I did not even possess a driving licence. All I was waiting for was to take one more look at the Quaid-e-Azam. I was hoping he would appear any moment now. Then suddenly there he was on the porch. Everyone came to attention, while I slunk to one side. Next to him stood his tall and graceful sister, Fatima, whose pictures I had often seen in newspapers and magazines. Standing a few steps away at a respectful distance from the Quaid was his secretary Matloob sahib [Matloob Hussain Syed].

'The Quaid adjusted his monocle and scrutinized each candidate carefully. His monocled eye came to rest on me. I shrank even more. Then I heard his penetrating voice: "You . . ." That much English I understood, but who was "you"? I was sure it was the man standing next to me, so I nudged him. "He has called for you." My companion stammered, "Sahib, I?" The Quaid-e-Azam's voice rose again: "No . . . you." His thin but steel-like finger was pointed at me. I began to tremble. "Sir, I?" "Yes," he replied. This one word went through me like a bullet out of a Royal Enfield .303 rifle. My throat, from which I had raised so many slogans for the Quaid, was now utterly dry. I could not speak. He took off his monocle and said, "All right." It seemed to me that he had somehow come to know how I felt and in order to end my agony had said, "All right." He turned, looked at his young and handsome secretary, said something to him and then went back into the house with his sister. I was about to run off when Matloob spoke: "Sahib has asked that you report here tomorrow at ten." I could not even ask him why I had been called, nor could I tell him that I had no qualifications for the job the Quaid-e-Azam had advertised for. I could not. Then Matloob sahib walked back into the house and I returned home.

'Next morning, I duly reported at the house and was informed by the Quaid's secretary that the sahib had liked me and I was to immediately take charge of the garage. My first thought was that I should confess that I knew nothing and that the Quaid-e-Azam had been misled. I had walked in just like that and was in no position to take the responsibility being given to me, but I don't know why I just kept quiet. I was given the keys to the garage and put in charge of the Quaid's four cars. The only car I had driven off and on was Seth Ardeshir Irani's Buick and that too on a straight road. The Malabar Hill was full of hair-raising bends and turns and I, poor Azad, was now required to drive a man on whose life depended the survival of millions of Muslims, all along this hazardous route and God alone knew where else.

'I had a wild urge to drop the keys on the ground and run all the way home, pick up my things and get on a train bound for Delhi, but thought better of it. It would be best to tell Jinnah sahib the truth, ask his forgiveness and go back to where I belonged, I said to myself. However, believe me, such an opportunity did not come my way for six months.'

'How?' I asked Mohammad Hanif Azad.

'This is how it was,' he explained. 'I was informed six months after I had joined that I was to drive the car to the porch and wait. I almost fainted but consoled myself with the thought that as soon as the Quaid appeared I would salute him, hand over the keys of the garage to him and then fall at his feet. That did not happen. The moment he walked out to the porch, I was so dumbfounded that I could not utter a single word. Fatima sahiba, his sister, was also with him, and Manto sahib, how can you fall at someone's feet in a woman's presence? It wouldn't have been right somehow. So Manto sahib I had to start the car, a new Packard it was. I silently prayed to God and managed to drive it out on the road through the front gate without a hitch. I negotiated all the turns of the Malabar Hill quite well, but when I came to the red light on the main road, I ran into trouble. My master Buddhan had taught me to use the brake gently, but I was so nervous that when I yanked it down, the car came to a stop so suddenly and with such a jolt that the cigar the Quaid was smoking fell out of his hand and Fatima sahiba was practically thrown out of her seat. She began to curse me and I thought I would die. My hands began to tremble and I felt my head reeling. The Quaid-e-Azam picked up his cigar from the floor and said something in English, which I thought meant I should return to the residence. Once we got back, he asked for another car and another driver and drove off. My next opportunity to serve him did not come until six months later.'

'And you served him the same way?' I asked, smiling.

Azad smiled too. 'Well, the thing was that sahib did not try me all this time. There were other drivers who were used. They all wore sahib's livery and very smart it was. Matloob sahib would inform us the night before who the driver for the next day was going to be and which car was to be taken out. Off and on, I would ask about myself but he would say nothing. The fact was that nobody could say with certainty what the sahib had in mind, nor did anyone dare ask him. He was very matter-of-fact and would only speak when it was necessary to speak, and listened only to that which was necessary to listen to. That was why despite being physically close to the Quaid, I could never find out why he had chucked me aside in his garage as a useless spare.'

I ventured a guess: 'Maybe he had forgotten all about you.' Azad laughed loudly. 'No, sir, no way the sahib had forgotten or would forget anything. He well knew that Azad had been feasting for the last six months without doing the least bit of work. And Manto sahib when Azad feasts away, it takes a lot to keep him happy. Just look at me and my big body.'

I looked at him. He was indeed a big and strong man. I could imagine what he must have been in the year 1937 or 1938. Since I had learnt that he had once been the Quaid's chauffeur, I had been looking for an opportunity to talk to him. I was to meet him several times and ask him about his days with the Quaid. As I began to write this account, it occurred to me that the Quaid-e-Azam liked strength, as Allama Mohammad Iqbal, the poet, liked tall people. The Quaid's choice of those who worked for him was governed by this basic consideration: strength. During Azad's time, everyone who worked for the Quaid was physically strong and good-looking. Matloob, his secretary, was well built and handsome, as were the drivers and the security guards. Mr Jinnah may have been physically weak but he had nerves of steel. It makes psychological sense that he did not wish to be associated with weaklings. One always takes good care of what one likes. The Quaid was no different. He was very particular about the smart turnout of his staff. The Pathan watchman was under orders to always wear his traditional dress. Azad, though not a Punjabi, was often asked to wear a turban because it made men look tall and impressive. If his turban was well and properly tied, he would sometimes earn himself a special tip.

Come to think of it, the secret of Quaid-e-Azam's strong character lay in his physical infirmity. He was always conscious of his fragility and it was this awareness that was his greatest strength. It manifested itself in everything, from the way he carried himself to how he spoke. Azad told me that the Quaid-e-Azam ate very little. 'He was such a small eater that I would often wonder what it was that kept him alive. Had I been put on that diet, I would have begun to vanish in a matter of days. Every day, four to five chickens were prepared in the kitchen and all Jinnah sahib ate would be a small bowl of soup. Fresh fruit would come to the house in large quantities every day but he would hardly eat any; it all went into the servants' bellies. Every day before going to sleep, he would indicate from a list what he wished to be prepared the next day. I would be handed a hundred-rupee note to cover the shopping.'

'A hundred rupees every day?' I asked Azad.

'Yes sir, one hundred rupees. The Quaid-e-Azam never asked us to account for it. What was not spent would be divided among the staff. On some days, it would be thirty rupees, on others forty and sometimes even sixty or seventy. He certainly knew about it but he never once asked for accounts. Miss Jinnah, however, was different and would often say that we were all thieves and were charging more for our shopping than what we had paid. We would listen to her quietly because we knew that the sahib did not really care about such things. On such occasions, he would tell his sister, "It's all right, it's all right."

'However, there was one occasion when it did not turn out to be "all right" and Miss Jinnah was so angry with the cooks that she laid off both of them. One was exclusively assigned to cook European meals, while the other was in charge of Indian cuisine. The latter would often be idle, sometimes for months on end. When his turn came, he would spring into action, but the Quaid-e-Azam was not really overly fond of Indian food. He kept quiet when both cooks were sacked because he would never interfere in his sister's affairs. For several days, both of them would go to the Taj to eat their meals. This was great as far as we were concerned. We would take the cars out in search of new cooks and gallivant around the city royally, only to come back and report that we had failed to find anyone suitable. In the end, Miss Jinnah asked the two old cooks to come back.

'Small eaters are either jealous of those who eat more than they do or are happy to see them eat well. The Quaid fell in the latter category of small eaters. That was why he never asked us what we had done with the money we had obviously not spent on meat and groceries. Let me tell you a story. The year was 1939. I was gently driving the Quaid in his white Packard along the Marine Drive, the waves beating languidly against the shore. There was a touch of cold in the air. I could see that Jinnah sahib was in a pleasant mood. I thought it was a good opportunity to mention the Id festival, which was around the corner. I could see him in my rear-view mirror. There was a faint smile on his lips. He knew what I meant. I wanted some money. His faithful cigar was between his lips. Finally, he spoke, "Well, well, you have suddenly become a Muslim . . . try being a bit of a Hindu for a while." Only four days earlier, the Quaid had tipped me two hundred rupees and thus made a good Muslim out of me, which was why he was now advising me to embrace a bit of Hinduism since I wanted more money.'

The Quaid-e-Azam's domestic life has always been a mystery and will remain so. It has been generally said that his domestic life was non-existent because all his time was taken up by politics. He had lost his wife years earlier and his daughter had married a Parsi against his express wishes.

Azad told me, 'This was a great shock for the sahib because he wanted her to marry a Muslim, no matter what caste or colour he was, but his daughter would argue with him. She would say that if he himself had exercised his freedom to choose a wife why was he not willing to accord the same freedom to her?'

The Quaid-e-Azam had married the daughter of a prominent Bombay Parsi, something that had been deeply resented by the Parsi community, which wanted the slight avenged. Some people said that the marriage of the Quaid's daughter to a Parsi was the result of a well-thought-out plan. When I mentioned this to Azad, his reaction was, 'God knows best, but all I know is that after his wife's death, this came as the greatest shock to the Quaid-e-Azam. When he learnt of the marriage, you could see the grief on his face. He was very transparent that way. You could know how he felt by merely looking at him. He was a sensitive man and even a minor incident could upset him. His brow would furrow and you would know that he was angry or upset. Only he could measure the extent of his grief, but those who saw him during those days knew how restless he was. For two weeks, he would not receive visitors. He would just keep smoking his cigars and pacing up and down in his room. He must have walked hundreds of miles in those two weeks.

'He would always pace about the room when he was thinking, often late at night, all alone, up and down the spotless floor of his room, taking measured steps. His brown-and-white or black-and-white brogues would produce a rhythmic pattern of sound as the night wore on. It was like a clock ticking. The Quaid-e-Azam loved his shoes. Was it because they were always at his feet and would do exactly what he willed?

'After two weeks he resurfaced. There was no sign of grief on his face, nor any tension. His head was again held high, although for two weeks he had tended to keep it bent. But this did not mean he had forgotten what had happened or really recovered from it.'

I asked Azad how he knew that. 'Nothing is hidden from servants,' he replied. 'He would sometimes ask for a certain metal chest to be brought to his room and unlocked. It was full of clothes that belonged to his dead wife and his headstrong daughter when she was a little girl. The clothes would be taken out and sahib would gaze at them without saying a word. His gaunt, transparent face would become clouded. "It's all right, it's all right," he would say, then remove his monocle, wipe it and walk away.

'The Quaid had three sisters, Fatima, Rehmat and a third one whose name I do not remember. They used to live in Dongri. Rehmat Jinnah lived at Chowpati Corner near Chinoy Motor Works. Her husband was employed somewhere and did not earn much. Sahib would give me a sealed envelope every month with money in it, and sometimes a packet, which probably contained clothes. These I had to deliver to Rehmat Jinnah. Off and on, sahib and Miss Jinnah would go and visit her. The other sister who lived in Dongri was married too and, as far as I knew, was well off and in no need of financial assistance. The Quaid had a brother whom he used to help regularly, but he was not allowed to come to the house. I once saw him in Bombay. It was at the Savoy bar. He looked like the Quaid and he had just ordered a small rum. He had the same nose, the same general features, the same combed hair with a grey streak in the middle. When I asked someone who that person was, I was told it was Mr Muhammad Ali Jinnah's brother, Ahmad Ali. I watched him for a long time. He sipped his rum slowly and paid the bill—which was less than a rupee—with a flourish as if it was a vast sum of money. The way he sat there, you would have thought he was not in a third-class Bombay watering hole but the Taj Mahal Hotel itself. Before the historic Gandhi–Jinnah meeting, there was an equally historic meeting of Bombay Muslims, which a friend of mine attended. He told me that as the Quaid-e-Azam spoke in his characteristic style, in a back corner stood his brother, Ahmad Ali, muttering, a monocle fitted to his eye.

'The only indoor sport the Quaid-e-Azam liked was billiards. Whenever the urge to play came upon him, he would order the billiards room to be opened and although it used to be cleaned and dusted every day, the servants would still take one extra look at everything on such days to be sure that all was spick and span. I was permitted to go to the billiards room because I too had a bit of a liking for the game. Twelve balls would be placed in front of the sahib and he would carefully choose three and then begin playing. Miss Jinnah would often be there too. Sahib would place his cigar between his lips and study the position of the ball that he planned to hit. This would take several minutes, as he would examine it from every angle. He would weigh the cue in his hand, run it over his long and slim fingers as if it was a bow he was going to play a stringed instrument with, take aim and then stop short of executing the stroke because he had thought of a better angle. He only played his shot when he was fully satisfied that it was the right one. If the shot went through as planned, he would smile triumphantly at his sister.

'In politics, the Quaid-e-Azam was equally meticulous. He never made a hasty decision. As at billiards, he would examine the situation from every angle and only move when he was sure he would get it right the first time. He would take the measure of his quarry and choose the right weapon to bring it down. He was not one of those who would hurriedly pick up a gun and shoot without looking, confident that they would not miss. The Quaid was mindful of every pitfall before going into attack.'

According to Azad, the Quaid-e-Azam avoided casual visitors because he hated idle talk. 'He only had ears for relevant and brief conversation. In the special room where he received visitors, there was only one sofa with a small side table. He would flick the ash from his cigar in an ashtray that lay on that table. There were two glass-front cabinets resting against the opposite wall where he kept copies of the Holy Quran presented to him by his admirers. His personal papers were also kept here. Most of his time was spent in that room. If one of us was sent for, we were expected to stand at the door and listen to his instructions. Then we would leave. The papers he was looking at would lie scattered on the sofa. If he wanted to have a letter written, he would send for Matloob or his stenographer and dictate it in a harsh, decisive voice. Although my knowledge of English was limited, I always felt that he emphasized words that did not need emphasis.'

The harshness Azad refers to was perhaps an unconscious defensive reaction to his physical frailty. His life was like a bubble on moving waters but he gave the world the appearance of a giant whirlpool. It was his lack of physical strength that kept him alive so long. Azad said the Quaid's best friend, with whom he had the most informal relations, was the late Nawab Bahadur Yar Jang. 'He would often come to stay and the two would talk for hours on national and political issues. The Quaid was a different person when he was with the Nawab. He was the only man with whom he talked as one talks to a close, personal friend. They were like two childhood buddies. When they were together in a room, you would often hear them laughing loudly. There were others who came to visit, including Raja Sahib of Mahmoodabad, I.I. Chundrigar, Maulana Zahid Hussain, Nawabzada Liaquat Ali Khan, Nawab Sir Mohammad Ismail and Ali Imam. However, the sahib dealt with them in an official kind of way. Gone was that easy informality which one associated with Bahadur Yar Jang's visits.'

I asked Azad if Liaquat was a frequent visitor.

'Yes, he was,' Azad answered. 'The Quaid treated him as his most talented pupil. Liaquat would show the utmost deference to him and carry out his orders to the last detail. Sometimes when he had been sent for, he would ask me before being shown in what kind of a mood the sahib was in. I would always tell him because when the Quaid was in a bad mood everyone knew, even the walls of the Malabar Hill home. The Quaid-e-Azam was particular about the appearance and conduct of his servants and staff. He hated everything that lacked cleanliness, including human character. He liked Matloob very much but when he learnt that he was carrying on with a Muslim League woman volunteer, he was annoyed because he was not one to tolerate such deviant behaviour. Matloob was called in, questioned and sent home. However, whenever the Quaid met him later, he always treated him like an old friend.

'Once I came home very late. You see I had gone out to town and spent quite a few hours at a bar. I thought the sahib would not know how late I had been, but I was wrong. He sent for me the next day and told me in English that I was spoiling my character, then added in broken Urdu, "Well, *ab hum tumhara shadi banai ga*"—We will have to get you married off now. Four months later when he came to Delhi from Bombay to attend a meeting of the Muslim League, as desired by him, I was duly married. It was because of my association with him that I found a wife who came from a Syed family. I was a Sheikh by caste but had been accepted as a son-in-law by the Syeds because I was in the service of the Quaid-e-Azam.'

I asked Azad if he had ever heard the Quaid-e-Azam say 'I am sorry.' Azad shook his head. 'No, I am sure if the words had ever escaped his lips, he would have excised them from the dictionary for good.' This one observation contains the key to Quaid-e-Azam Mohammad Ali Jinnah's character, I think.

Mohammad Hanif Azad is alive in the Pakistan that his Quaid-e-Azam gifted to him, a country that is trying to survive in a harsh world under the leadership of his talented pupil, Liaquat Ali Khan. On this piece of free land, he sits on a broken cot outside the office of Punjab Art Pictures, close to a betel-leaf seller, and waits for his sahib and prays for the day when he will be paid his salary on time. He is even prepared to become a bit of a Hindu, just as the Quaid-e-Azam had advised, provided there is an opportunity.

Last time I spoke to him about the Quaid, he was depressed. I realized that he did not have enough on him to buy himself even a betel leaf. I talked to him of this and that and managed to get his mind off his troubles.

He sighed. 'My sahib is dead. How I wish I was with him on his last journey, driving his white Packard with the roof down. How I wish I could have driven him gently to his destination. His delicate temperament was not suited for a rough, jolting ride. I have heard—and I do not know if it is true or untrue—that when his plane brought him to Karachi, on what was to be his last trip, the ambulance that was to take him to the Governor General's house broke down. The engine stalled after it had gone a short distance. I know how much that must have upset my sahib.'

There were tears in Azad's eyes.

A GIRL FROM DELHI

The religious killings had shown no sign of abating. India had been partitioned, but the bloodletting continued: Hindus killing Muslims, Muslims killing Hindus.

So one day, Nasim Akhtar, the young and much-sought-after nautch girl from Delhi's 'red light' quarter, said to her old mother, 'Let's get out of here.'

The old woman carefully placed a betel leaf in her toothless mouth and asked, 'But where will we go, sweetheart?'

'Pakistan,' Nasim Akhtar replied, and looked at her music teacher, old Ustad Achhan Khan. 'Khan sahib, what do you think? Is it any longer safe for us Muslims to live in Delhi?'

Achhan Khan had perhaps been thinking along the same lines, because he immediately said, 'You are quite right, but we must have your mother's—our burri baiji's—permission.'

But that was the difficult bit. Despite Nasim Akhtar's fervent pleading, the old woman would not go along. One day, the young woman told her mother, 'It is going to be Hindu raj; they don't want any Muslims around.'

'So what,' her mother replied. 'We are in business because of our Hindu patrons and clients. All your admirers and regulars are Hindus, don't you forget that. There's nothing the Muslims can do for us or that we want from them, I am telling you.'

'Don't say that mother,' Nasim Akhtar reacted sharply. 'The Quaid-e-Azam, Jinnah sahib, has worked so hard and got us our own country, Pakistan, and that's where we should go and live.'

In his opium-saturated voice, Mando the musician chipped in, 'Chotti bai, may God protect you, what a wonderful thing you have said! I am prepared to go to Pakistan this very minute. If I die there and my bones are placed in its earth, my soul will rest in eternal peace.'

The other musicians were also equally enthusiastic about moving to Pakistan, but since the burri bai was against the idea, no more was said about it.

The burri bai, herself the toast of Delhi in her youth, sent a message to Seth Gobind Prakash, one of Nasim Akhtar's ardent and rich admirers and a frequent visitor to the kotha. The message conveyed that her daughter was terrified of all this Hindu–Muslim business and would he kindly come and set her mind at rest?

He came the next morning and Nasim Akhtar's mother said to him, 'Please talk to her. This girl wants us all to move to Pakistan, but I have been trying to reason with her. With such kind and generous friends as yourself, why should we leave Delhi? In fact, I have no doubt that in Pakistan we will be reduced to sweeping the streets. Sethji, I need a favour from you.'

The seth, who was only half-listening to the burri bai as his mind was elsewhere, asked, 'Ah, yes, what is that?'

'Could you have two or three armed guards posted outside our kotha for a few days so that this girl can feel safe?'

'No trouble at all. I can speak to the chief of police right away, so don't you worry. He will post a special police guard for your place, by this very evening, I promise,' the seth said expansively.

'May God bless you!' said the burri bai, much moved.

'Perhaps I will drop in myself this evening. Wouldn't it be nice to see our Nasim Akhtar's mujra?'

The old courtesan rose. 'Yes, indeed, this is your own place and this girl is always here at your service. Also, you must dine here tonight, seth sahib.'

'Unfortunately, I am on a diet these days,' he said, running his hands over his big belly.

After the seth's departure, the house was given a thorough cleaning. The big floor cushions, on which the clients reclined as they sat and watched Nasim Akhtar perform, had their covers changed, new lights were installed and a special tin of scarce cigarettes was ordered for Seth Gobind Prakash.

While the final touches were still being given to these elaborate preparations, the servant burst into the room, his face white with fear. He even had difficulty speaking, but finally managed to tell them that he had seen five Sikhs pounce on a Muslim street vendor just around the corner and stab him to death in the most gruesome manner.

Nasim Akhtar nearly fainted when she heard what had happened. Ustad Achhan Khan made gallant efforts to reassure her but she was just too shaken by what she had heard. Finally her mother said, 'This is not the first time a man has been killed in the street; these things are always going on. Now, child, don't you think it is time you got ready for the evening? Seth sahib could be here any minute.'

Although that was the last thing she felt like doing, Nasim Akhtar put on her silks and brocades, her peshwaz, painted her face, did her hair and took her customary place in the room where all the entertaining was done. But she couldn't get over that poor Muslim street vendor lying dead in a pool of blood. She wanted to throw off her ornaments, get out of her shimmering clothes, put on something plain and beg her mother to listen to her because she was sure something terrible was going to happen to them.

Finally she told her mother what had been going through her mind, but the old woman merely replied, 'Why should anything happen to us? We haven't offended anybody.'

'And who had that poor vendor offended? They killed him nevertheless, didn't they?' Nasim Akhtar said gravely. 'They cut him into pieces. It is the bad ones who escape and the innocent who get killed.'

'You don't know what you are saying,' her mother retorted irately.

'Who *does* these days? All I know is that blood is flowing in the streets of Delhi,' the young woman said. Then she rose, walked to the balcony and surveyed the street below. She saw four men with guns. She waved to Ustad Achhan Khan to come and take a look. 'Are they the armed policemen seth sahib had promised to arrange?' she asked him.

'They don't look like police to me; they are not wearing uniforms. They look like goondas to me,' the old man whispered.

'Goondas!' Nasim Akhtar nearly screamed.

'God only knows. They are coming towards the kotha. Nasim, I think you should take the stairs and go to the rooftop and I'll follow you in a few minutes. There is definitely something very wrong here.'

Nasim Akhtar slunk out of the room. The old woman had not noticed. Ustad Achhan Khan followed soon after. Nasim Akhtar's heart was sinking. 'What is going on?' she asked the old man.

'Just what I had feared. The four men came up as soon as you had left the room. They said they had been sent by Seth Gobind Prakash to fetch you to his residence since he couldn't make it himself. Your mother was pleased and said it was very kind of him. She thought you were in the bathroom. She told the men she would have to come along too, but one of them said, "We don't want you, you old hag. We have come for the young one." 'When I heard that, I slipped out and rushed here to warn you,' the old man said breathlessly.

'What should we do?' Nasim Akhtar asked desperately.

Ustad Achhan Khan scratched his head. 'Let me think of something. Perhaps we should get out of here as fast as we can.'

'And my mother?' she asked.

'God will protect her, but we should escape while there is time,' he replied after a pause.

The adjoining roof, a few feet lower, was that of the local laundry. Without much difficulty, they jumped on to it. Luckily, there were stairs leading from the roof to the street and in a few minutes they were safely out. They walked a block or two and found a tonga owned by a Muslim who agreed to take them to the railway station.

On their way, they saw an army truck with Muslim soldiers who were evacuating people from Hindu areas and taking them to the station where special refugee trains for Pakistan were being run. They got a ride and were in time to board a train going to Lahore in Pakistan, where they arrived the next morning.

They were taken to a refugee camp in a place outside the city called Walton. They lived there for a few weeks and then Ustad Achhan Khan sold some of Nasim Akhtar's jewellery and they moved to a small, inexpensive hotel. After a few days, the old man rented a kotha in Hira Mandi, Lahore's famous 'red light' courtesan district.

One day Ustad Achhan Khan said to her, 'I think we need to invest in some purchases, I mean musical instruments, floor cushions, that sort of thing, and with God's blessings, we can take up where we left off in Delhi.'

But to his surprise, Nasim Akhtar replied, 'No, Khan sahib, my heart is not in that sort of thing any more. I don't even want to live in this neighbourhood. Please find me a small place in some nice, normal locality. Delhi is behind me. That life for me is finished. I just want to live like a normal woman.'

'What are you talking about, girl?' Achhan Khan asked.

'That was all a long time ago. I don't even want to think about those days. Please pray for me; may God give me the strength to make a break from my past.' Nasim Akhtar's eyes were full of tears.

Over the next few days, Ustad Achhan Khan tried his best to talk her out of her strange resolve but her mind really seemed to be made up. One day she said to him, 'I would like to get married, that is, if someone would have me; otherwise I will remain a spinster.'

Achhan Khan could not understand what had happened to her. Was it the partition of the country that had unhinged her? Women in this profession were not like this. But he soon gave up on her. She really had changed. He found her a small house in a quiet locality, far away from Hira Mandi; but he moved back to the area himself, where he felt at home, and was hired by a rich and popular courtesan as her music teacher.

Nasim Akhtar was happy. It was a hard life, but that was what she wanted. A young boy-servant did her shopping and helped her around the house. The money from the sale of the rest of her ornaments was enough to keep her going for some time yet. She had become very religious, praying five times a day, and abstaining from food and drink during Ramadan.

Over the last couple of months, an old woman called Jannatey had begun to visit her off and on. Nasim Akhtar was grateful for her company; what she did not know was that this woman was a procuress who enticed young girls and sold them into prostitution. If they had a talent for song and dance, they became rich courtesans; otherwise they became part of Hira Mandi's infamous flesh trade.

One day, while Jannatey was out in the courtyard, she heard Nasim Akhtar singing most beautifully as she washed her hair. She had not sung for a long time and even now was not conscious of the fact that she was singing. By instinct and experience the old woman knew the moment she heard the singing that this strange girl from Delhi who never talked and lived alone could find a place in Hira Mandi, where she could become one of Lahore's leading singing girls. The question was how to go about it.

She tried a number of ruses, made some indirect, some direct references to the possibility, but none of them worked. Finally, one day, she threw her arms around Nasim Akhtar and kissed her on the forehead affectionately. 'Daughter, I beg of you, don't misunderstand me. I was only testing you, but you are a young woman of great piety and virtue, and not for you those things. I am sorry.'

Nasim Akhtar was taken in; she even told the old woman that she wanted to get married to a nice and simple man as it was not safe or advisable for a young woman to be living all alone without anyone to look after her.

This was just the opening Jannatey had been looking for. 'You leave that to me; I will find you the perfect husband, a man who will worship you.'

In the next few days, the old procuress brought Nasim Akhtar a number of fake proposals, making none of them sound too good, until one day she burst into the house announcing that she had found the man she was looking for. He was not too old, had a lot of property, was of a fine, upright moral character, and if Nasim Akhtar would trust her, she would go right ahead with the arrangements.

Nasim Akhtar was mentally prepared for any proposal that sounded good, more so because she had complete faith in the old woman. So she said Jannatey could proceed with the arranged marriage. She did not need to see or meet the man.

A date was set and a simple ceremony took place and Nasim Akhtar was married. She was happy that she had found a good husband who would look after her. However, her happiness was not to last beyond twenty-four hours, because the very next day she overheard her husband talking to two old courtesans from Hira Mandi. They were haggling over her price. She was being sold off. Jannatey was the mediator.

Nasim Akhtar rushed into her bedroom, tears running down her cheeks. She cried for a long time, then she dried her eyes and unpacked the clothes she had brought with her from Delhi, the ones she had been wearing that last evening, and quietly walked out of the house, making straight for the kotha where Ustad Achhan Khan was employed.

THE GREAT DIVIDE

The 1947 upheavals came and went, much like the few bad days you get in an otherwise sunny Punjabi winter. Karim Dad lived through them, refusing to be cowed down. The will of God it might have been, as they said, but he was not one to surrender. He had fought many brave encounters during the last few months, not because he wanted to inflict defeat on anyone, but because it seemed to him that if you gave in you were less than a man.

At least, that is how he appeared to others; he had never thought consciously about these things. Had someone actually asked him in so many words if surrender to the enemy was a negation of one's manhood, he would have been confused, as if he had been told to solve an intricate mathematical equation.

Karim Dad was not interested in adding, subtracting or multiplying things. The 1947 upheavals were over. He took no interest in the balance sheets everyone was busy drawing up now. How many dead? How much in property losses? All he knew was that he had lost his father, Rahim Dad. He had carried his father's dead body over his shoulder and buried him near a well in a grave he had dug with his own hands in the soft earth.

A great deal had happened in their village. Hundreds of young and old people had been killed. Scores of girls had gone missing; others had been brutally raped. Those whom the upheavals had affected directly would not be able to forget their misfortune or the cruelty of the enemy for a long time.

As for Karim Dad, he had shed no tears. In fact, he was proud of the bravery of his father who had fought nearly thirty armed men single-handed, till he fell. All Karim Dad had said when he had been told about his father's death was, 'He should have listened to me. Didn't I tell him one must keep at least one weapon on one's person these days?'

Then he had gone out, picked up his father's body from the fields where it lay and buried it next to a well. His last words to him were, 'Only God knows about good and bad deeds, but may you end up in paradise.'

Rahim Dad, who was not only Karim's father but his best friend as well, had been killed mercilessly. The villagers even now became angry and abusive when they mentioned his killers, but Karim Dad had never said a word. His standing crop had been burnt to the ground, two of his houses had been gutted, but he had never once tried to recount his losses. The nearest he had come to doing that was, 'Whatever happened was because of our own mistakes.' He had never gone into details.

The village was still busy mourning those terrible days when Karim Dad married Jeena, a girl he had had his eye on for some time. She had lost her only brother in the riots. He was a giant of a man and the only one she had in the world after her parents died. Though Jeena loved Karim Dad as much as a woman can love a man, this love now lay buried under her grief for her dead brother. She would cry often.

Karim Dad hated people crying or feeling sorry for themselves. He hated to see Jeena in mourning, though he never told her that. She was a woman and he was afraid he might hurt her. However, one day when they were working in the fields, he couldn't contain himself. 'It is one year since we buried the dead. Even they by now must be tired of your mourning. Try to get over it. Save your tears; God knows how many more we are fated to mourn while we are alive.'

At first, Jeena had felt offended, but because she loved him, she finally convinced herself that Karim Dad was right. When word had first leaked out in the village that Karim Dad was planning to marry Jeena, the elders had opposed it. However, it was a feeble kind of opposition, because the fact was that the people were so sick of mourning the dead that they just didn't have the will to take a stand on the issue. So the wedding had gone ahead and it had been a lot of fun. It was after a long time that the village had seen a bride.

This was the first happy thing to have happened since the

upheavals of Partition and the celebrations were spontaneous. To some it almost felt like a ghost wedding, so unused had they become to lights and laughter. When one of Karim Dad's friends mentioned this to him, he thought it was the funniest thing he had ever heard. He even told Jeena, but she did not think it was funny. In fact, a shudder ran through her body.

On their first night together, Karim Dad took hold of Jeena's bangled wrist and said, 'This ghost is going to haunt you for the rest of your life. Even Rahim Sain, the village witch doctor, will discover that his mumbo-jumbo does not work on the ghost called Karim Dad.'

Jeena put her hennaed finger between her teeth and blushed. 'Keemay, is there nothing you are afraid of?' Touching his moustache with the tip of his tongue, he said, 'Is fear anything to be afraid of, silly?' They laughed.

Jeena had almost forgotten the tragedies of the past. Her mind was now on her baby because she was pregnant. Karim Dad would look at her and say, 'I swear by God, you never looked more beautiful; but if you have put on this special look for that one you are carrying, then I'm telling you, he has a rival . . . me.'

Jeena would blush, try to cover her protruding belly with her dupatta and Karim Dad would laugh. 'Don't hide this thief. Don't I know all the things you are doing behind my back for this little swine!'

Jeena's face would darken. 'Don't abuse him.'

'He is a little swine because I am a big swine myself,' Karim Dad would say, bellowing with laughter.

The festival of Chotti Id came, followed by the Burri Id, both of which Karim Dad celebrated with great gusto. It was twelve days before the last Burri Id when the village had been attacked and his father, Rahim Dad, and her brother, Fazal Elahi, were killed. Jeena had wept bitterly remembering their deaths but Karim Dad was not one to let past sorrows darken his present.

Jeena found it hard to believe sometimes that she was beginning to forget such a great tragedy in her life. She didn't remember the deaths of her mother and father, but her brother, Fazal Elahi, who was six years older than her had become both father and mother to her. She also knew that it was because of her that he had not married and it was known to the entire village that he had laid down his life to save her honour. His death was the greatest tragedy in Jeena's life. It was like doomsday that had come to pass exactly twelve days before Burri Id. And now when she thought of it, she felt surprised at how quickly that great trauma had begun to be forgotten.

When the month of Muharram arrived, for the first time Jeena asked Karim Dad to fulfil her one ardent desire. She wanted to watch the Muharram procession go past with its riderless horse and commemorative floats. She had heard a lot about this from her friends. So she said to Karim Dad, 'Will you take me to watch the Muharram procession go by if I am well?'

'I'll take you even if you are not well . . . and that little swine too,' he replied with a wink.

For some time now there had been rumours that a war would break out between India and Pakistan. Actually, the moment Pakistan was born, it somehow seemed to have been decreed that there would be a war. When it would take place, no one in the village could say. If someone asked Karim Dad, he always had this cryptic answer: 'It will be when it will be, why waste time worrying about it now?'

Jeena had also heard the rumours and she was terrified. She hated violence; she had seen enough of it in her young life; she did not wish to see any more.

Meanwhile, Karim Dad had bought a gun and trained himself to become an expert marksman. He was strong and he was brave. When he was with her, she never felt any fear, but when she was with other women, she felt very scared.

Bakhto, the village midwife, who came regularly to look at Jeena, one day brought the news that the Indians were going to dam the rivers that brought water to their villages in the Punjab. Jeena did not understand what this meant, so when Karim Dad came home that evening, she said to him, 'They are saying that the Indians are going to take away our water. Why would they do that?'

'So that our lands turn to waste,' he replied matter-of-factly.

'But that is cruel,' she said, quite convinced now that the rumours were correct.

'Was Bakhto here today?' he asked.

'Yes.'

'And?'

'She said the baby would come in ten days.'

'Zindabad,' Karim Dad shouted gleefully.

'You are rejoicing. God knows what is going to happen to us,' Jeena answered.

Karim Dad went out, spending the rest of the evening gossiping with the other men in the village common. Chaudhry Nathoo, the headman, was there trying his best to answer all the anxious questions being put to him. There were some who were abusing Pandit Nehru; others were cursing India. Though not one man was prepared to believe that the rivers could actually be dammed and diverted.

'Which rivers are they going to dam?' Jeena had earlier asked Bakhto.

'The ones that irrigate our lands,' the midwife had replied.

'You can't be serious, auntie,' Jeena had said. 'No one can dam rivers; they are not drains, they are rivers.'

Bakhto, who was massaging her belly, had replied, 'I don't know girl, but I have told you what I heard. They say it is in the newspapers.'

'What is in the newspapers?'

'That they are going to dam our rivers.' Then she had run her hand expertly over Jeena's belly and said, 'He should be here in ten days.'

Karim Dad had merely said, 'Well, that's what they say,' when she asked him again about the rumours.

Some people in the village were of the view that this was a punishment from God and the only way of averting this catastrophe was to gather in the mosque and pray.

Nobody was abusing the Indians more than Chaudhry Nathoo.

It made Karim Dad squirm in his seat to hear the old man go on and on. 'It is mean and unfair; it is a bastardly act, a great sin, the greatest ever. It is what Yazid did when he dammed the river that brought water to Karbala where Hussain and his brave companions were fighting for survival. Many of them died of thirst, and that is what the Indians are doing.'

Karim Dad coughed two or three times, which meant that he wanted to say something. Chaudhry Nathoo had once again begun his tirade against the Indians, using the most filthy words he could think of. Suddenly, Karim Dad cut him short, 'Don't abuse them, Chaudhry.'

Chaudhry Nathoo, who was about to regale his audience with tales about the doubtful origin of the Indians and the morals of their mothers, couldn't believe his ears. 'What did you say?'

In a low but determined voice, Karim Dad replied, 'I said don't abuse them.'

Chaudhry Nathoo rasped back, 'What are they to you?' then addressed himself to the others, 'Did you hear that? He says I shouldn't abuse the Indians. Why don't you ask him what is his exact relationship to them? We would all like to know, I am sure.'

In a calm voice, Karim Dad replied, 'I'll tell you: they are my enemies.'

The headman laughed. 'Did you hear that! They are his enemies, he says, which means one should love one's enemies.'

'I didn't say one should love them. All I said was you shouldn't abuse them,' Karim Dad replied quietly.

'And why?' Miran Bux, one of Karim Dad's childhood friends, asked.

'What will you gain by that? They want to lay waste your lands and you think you will get even by abusing them. Is that wise? You only abuse when you have run out of other options,' Karim Dad said to Miran Bux.

'Do you have an option?'

'How can I answer this? It's not I alone who am involved, but hundreds upon thousands of others. How can I answer on their behalf? One has to think about these things coolly. They can't dam and divert our rivers in a couple of days; it will take them years, but you people will have vented all your anger in one day by abusing them.'

'He is talking nonsense,' Chaudhry Nathoo said.

'I am not talking nonsense. When it is war, everything is permissible. Haven't you seen two feuding wrestlers in a ring, fighting to the finish? There are no holds barred in such contests,' Karim Dad replied.

'You have a point there,' his friend said, scratching his head.

Karim Dad smiled. 'It follows then that they have every right to dam our rivers. It may appear to us as an act of cruelty, but it is no such thing to them. I think it is fair.'

'Fair, you said!' Chaudhry Nathoo screamed. 'When your tongue is hanging out because you have no water to drink, I will ask you if it is fair. When your children long for a mouthful of food, I will ask you if it is fair.'

'I will still say the same thing, Chaudhry,' Karim Dad replied. 'Why do you forget that it is not they alone who are our enemies; we are their enemies too. Had it been in our power, we would have seen to it that they received neither water to drink nor food to eat. I just don't think it is right to call the Indians mean, bastardly and cruel.'

'Hear that!' Chaudhry Nathoo shouted.

Karim Dad ignored him, turning to Miran Bux. 'It's foolish to expect your enemy to be kind to you. It is like complaining during battle that the other side is using heavier guns or bigger bombs compared to yours. What sort of a complaint is that?'

'But they are going to dam our waters and starve us, that is the issue. They want us to perish,' Chaudhry Nathoo said almost imploringly.

'Look Chaudhry Nathoo,' Karim Dad said, 'once you declare someone your enemy, then why complain that he is trying to starve you to death, that he is trying to turn your green fields into barren land? What do you expect him to do? Lay out a banquet for you?'

'You are talking nonsense,' was all that the headman could counter Karim Dad with.

But Karim Dad had not finished. 'It just so happens that the Indians are now in a position to take our water away from us. So, let's do something about it, instead of sitting here and abusing them. Don't expect the enemy to dig canals for you and fill them with milk and honey; expect him to poison your water so that you drink it and die. You will call it barbarism. I don't. If it is war, then it is a war, not a wedding contract with preconditions and the rest of it. You can't say, all right we will go to war, provided you don't starve us or take away our food. Or that if you must fire at us, use only a certain brand of cartridge. Be reasonable.'

'And how do I do that?' Chaudhry Nathoo asked.

Karim Dad did not answer, but rose and left.

He almost bumped into Bakhto as he walked through the front door. She was smiling. 'A boy like the new moon. Have you thought of a name?'

'Yes, I have,' he answered. 'Yazid, that's what he is going to be called.'

Bakhto's face went white because no Muslim child is ever called Yazid, as no Christian child can be called Judas. It is an evil name because it was Yazid on whose orders Hussain, the Prophet's grandson, and his companions were deprived of water and finally massacred.

Karim Dad ran into the house. Jeena was lying in bed, looking very pale. Next to her lay a tiny pink baby boy, his thumb in his mouth. Karim Dad touched him on the cheek. 'My little Yazid,' he said proudly.

'Yazid!' Jeena almost screamed.

'Yes, Yazid . . . that is his name,' Karim Dad said looking at the baby.

'What are you saying?' she asked in a shocked voice.

Karim Dad smiled. 'Yes, that's right, it is only a name after all.'

'But do you know whose name that is?' she asked.

'It is not necessary that this little one here should be the same Yazid. That Yazid dammed the waters; this one will make them flow again.'

BITTER HARVEST

When Qasim walked through the door, all he was conscious of was a burning pain in his thigh because of the embedded bullet. But when he saw the blood-soaked body of his wife lying in the courtyard, he forgot his pain. He wanted to grab his axe and rush out of the house, killing everyone who came in his path, smashing everything that caught his eye. Then he thought of his daughter, Sharifan.

'Sharifan! Sharifan!' he shouted.

The doors of the two rooms in the house were shut. Was she hiding behind one of them, he wondered. 'Sharifan! Sharifan!' he screamed. 'This is me, your father.' There was no answer. He pushed open the first door with both hands. What he saw was so horrifying that he almost fainted.

On the floor was the nearly naked body of a young girl, her small, upturned breasts pointing at the ceiling as she lay on her back. He wanted to scream but he couldn't. He turned his face away and said in a soft, grief-stricken voice, 'Sharifan.' Then he picked up some clothes from the floor and threw them over her. He did not notice that they had missed their target by several feet.

As he ran out of the house, axe in hand, he was no longer conscious of the bullet in his thigh or the blood-soaked body of his wife, but only of Sharifan, the naked Sharifan lying dead in a heap on the floor of her room.

Axe in hand, he began to move like molten lava through the deserted streets of the city. He saw a Sikh in the main square, a big hulk of a man, but so ferocious and sudden was Qasim's attack that the man fell to the ground like an uprooted tree, blood gushing out of his severed head.

Qasim could feel his own blood surging through his body, like boiling oil over which cold water is being sprinkled. He saw a group of five or six men at the far end of the road and moved towards them like an arrow. 'Har Har Mahadev,' they shouted, obviously taking him for a fellow Hindu. 'Motherfuckers,' he screamed and rushed at them, swinging his axe wildly.

In a few seconds, three of them had fallen to the ground in a blood-smeared pile; the others had run away. Like a man demented, he kept hitting them, till he fell on top of one of the dead bodies himself. He wasn't sure if he had fallen or been overpowered. He lay there waiting for the blow to come, but nothing happened. After a few minutes, he slowly opened his eyes. There was no one on the road, just three dead men among whom he lay.

He almost felt disappointed that he had not been killed, but then he remembered Sharifan's naked body, an image that seared his eyes like molten lead. He picked up his axe and was soon running through the streets, shouting obscenities.

The city was deserted. He turned randomly into a small side street, but was soon out of there when he realized that it was a Muslim neighbourhood. So far he had been hurling abuse at the mothers and sisters of his enemies; now he began to abuse their daughters.

He came to a stop in front of a small house. On the wooden door was a sign in Hindi. Qasim began to swing his axe at it and in a few minutes he had smashed the wood into a pulp. 'Come out, you bastards, come out!' he screamed as he went in.

One of the doors in the house creaked on its hinges and opened slowly to reveal a young girl. 'Who are you?' he asked. 'I am a Hindu,' she replied, running her tongue over her dry lips. She could not have been more than fourteen or fifteen.

Qasim threw away the axe and pounced on her like a wild beast, throwing her to the ground. Then he began to tear at her clothes and for half an hour he ravaged her like an animal gone berserk. There was no resistance; she had fainted.

When he finished, he realized that he was clutching her throat with both hands, his nails embedded into her soft skin. He released her with a violent jerk.

He closed his eyes and saw an image of his daughter, lying

dead on the floor, her small breasts pointing upwards. He broke into an icy sweat.

Through the smashed street door, a man ran into the house, a sword in his hand. He found Qasim squatting on the floor, trying to spread a blanket over someone lying there.

'Who are you?' the stranger roared.

Qasim turned his face towards him.

'Qasim!' the man screamed in disbelief.

Qasim blinked his eyes; his face wore a blank expression. He couldn't even see properly.

'What are you doing in my house?' the man shouted.

With a trembling finger, Qasim pointed to the blanket-covered heap on the floor. 'Sharifan,' he said in a hollow voice.

The other man pulled off the blanket. The sword fell from his hand; then he staggered out of the house wailing, 'Bimla, my daughter, Bimla.'

A BELIEVER'S VERSION

I swear by Allah . . . recite the Kalima . . . there is no God but Allah and Mohammed is His Prophet. You are all believers. You must believe what I tell you . . . I speak nothing but the truth . . . this has nothing to do with Pakistan . . . I can lay down my life for my beloved Quaid-e-Azam, the Great Leader, Muhammad Ali Jinnah, but this has nothing to do with Pakistan . . . I swear by God.

Please let's not be in a hurry . . . I know there are riots in the streets and you have little time for me, but in the name of God, I beseech you to hear me out . . . you've got to listen to my story . . . I have never denied murdering Tuka Ram. Yes, I ripped him open with a knife but I didn't kill him because he was a Hindu. Why did I kill him then? You have the right to know . . . but you must let me tell you the entire story.

I'll speak the truth and nothing but the truth . . . recite the Kalima . . . there is no God but Allah and Mohammed is His Prophet. May I die in sin, an infidel, if I did what I did knowing it would lead to this. The last time we had Hindu–Muslim trouble, I killed three Hindus but that was different. This Tuka Ram business was something else.

You are men of learning . . . you know all about women . . . the wise have said . . . beware of their wiles and, by God, they are right . . . if you don't hang me, I promise you I'll never go near a woman as long as I live . . . Oh God! What a fool I've been! Show me a woman and I get all worked up. Yes, yes, I know we all have to go one day to the Maker and He is going to ask questions . . . well, well, Inspector sahib, I'll be straight with you . . . the moment I set eyes on Rukma, I knew I was in for it. What a woman!

You'd be perfectly right to tell me that someone who earns

thirty-five rupees a month has absolutely no business running after women. I suppose I should have been doing my job, collecting rent, and keeping my nose clean. You see, I am a rent collector. But you should know how it all began. Flat 16 was where she lived. I had merely gone to collect the rent—all part of my monthly round. So I knock on the door and who opens it but Rukma Bai herself. I had seen her several times before but that day she looked ravishing. She had something flimsy on and her body shimmered. I think she had rubbed herself all over with oil. Oh God! I went crazy! I wanted to whip off that silly piece of cloth she had around her middle and start massaging her body—furiously. That was how it all began and before I knew it I was her slave.

What a woman! Her body was solid as a rock . . . I used to bruise myself making love to her . . . And she! Ah! She would say, 'A little harder, a little harder!'

Married? Yes, Inspector, the bitch was married. She even had another lover on the side, or so she claimed. Khan, the night watchman. Oh! I am going to spill the beans on her.

I was crazy about her . . . and she knew it because she would sometimes look at me sideways and smile . . . and when she did that, I swear to God, a chill ran down my spine . . . Oh! How I pined for her! Let me start at the beginning, shall I?

I was obsessed with her. All I wanted was that woman. I couldn't think of anything else. I was trapped and I knew it. My problem was that blasted toy-maker husband of hers. He was always in that one-room flat of theirs with those silly wooden toys of his. I just couldn't find the opportunity to sneak in to be with her.

And then I got a break. I was bumming around in the bazaar when I saw that man . . . what was he called? Yes, Girdhari. He was sitting on the pavement selling those wooden toys of his. And before you could blink your eyes, I was standing in front of Flat 16, my heart beating in my mouth. I knocked and she opened the door. I didn't know what to say. I almost turned and walked off but she smiled and called me in.

She closed the door, then asked me to sit down. 'I know what you are after but as long as Girdhari, my husband, is alive you can forget about it,' she said, the witch!

I stood up. She was so close to me, wearing the same flimsy excuse for a dress, her body glistening. Oh! I couldn't resist it any longer. I threw my arms around her. I was wild with excitement. 'I don't know what you are talking about,' I said. She embraced me right back. God, what a body that woman had, Inspector! But let me tell you my story.

'Girdhari can burn in hell,' I whispered, 'I want you.'

Rukma pushed me away. 'You don't want your nice clothes soiled by the oil on my body, do you?'

'I don't care what I soil,' I said as I grabbed her once again.

Inspector sahib, if you had lashed my back with a whip, I wouldn't have let go of her. 'Sit down,' she purred. 'Don't stand there. Come, I want to talk to you,' she told me. I was like putty in her hands. So there I was sitting, not saying a word. What was she planning? That sala, Girdhari, was in the bazaar selling toys, so what was she afraid of?

'Rukma,' I said breathlessly, 'There never will be an opportunity as good as this.'

She ran her fingers through my hair. 'There'll be better ones but you'll have to do something for me. Will you?'

Inspector sahib, I was not myself at the time. I didn't know what I was doing. Oh, the devil had taken hold of me. I told her, 'I'll kill fifteen men if you want me to.'

She smiled, the witch, and said, 'I believe you.'

I spent some more time with her. She fed me something she had cooked. We talked of this, that and the other, you know. Finally, she asked me to leave.

Ten days passed. On the eleventh, at two in the morning, someone woke me up gently. I sleep on the landing; yes, in the same building where Rukma lives. It was she. My heart leapt with excitement. 'Come with me,' she said softly. I followed her on tiptoe. She pushed her door open and I slipped in after her. I lunged for her; I just couldn't wait. 'Not yet,' she said, as she switched on the light. Someone was asleep on the floor, face covered. 'Who's that?' I asked in sign language. 'Sit down,' she answered. She ran her fingers lovingly through my hair but what she said next so casually made me break out in a cold sweat. And you know what she said?

Recite the Kalima . . . there is no God but Allah and Mohammed is His Prophet . . . I speak the truth and nothing but the truth . . . a woman like Rukma, I've never met in my entire life. You know what she told me with a smirk? 'I've killed Girdhari.' Just like that! With her bare hands she had killed a strong, well-built man like her husband. Some woman she was! As God is my witness, Inspector sahib, when I think of that night, I break out in goosebumps. She had garrotted him to death with wire rope. She had squeezed the last breath out of his body by twisting the wire rope around his neck with the aid of a small stick. The poor man's tongue was hanging out and his eyes had nearly popped out of their sockets. She said it hadn't taken long.

She insisted that I should see Girdhari's face. My blood froze when I looked at him but Rukma, she didn't bat an eye. Then she lay down only a few feet from the body and told me to lie next to her. I felt dead myself but then she did something to me, something very unexpected, and I was suddenly on fire. I'll never forget that night! There lay Girdhari and there lay the two of us, one on top of the other. What a night that was!

In the morning, quite methodically, Rukma and I cut Girdhari into three pieces with his very own tools. We must have made a bit of noise but the neighbours were used to Girdhari making his usual racket every morning as he got down to work. You may well ask, Inspector sahib, why I went along with this grisly business, why I didn't rush to the police and rat on her. I'll tell you why. That one night with her had me eating out of her hand. If she had asked me to go kill fifteen men, I would have gone right out and done that.

There was the question of getting rid of the body. All said and done, she was a woman and needed a hand there. 'Not to worry, darling,' I told her. 'We'll put Girdhari in a trunk and, as night falls, I'll take it out and dump it somewhere.' But God moves in strange ways. That day, Hindu–Muslim killings erupted in the city and a thirty-six-hour curfew was clamped on the worst-affected neighbourhoods. 'Abdul Karim,' I said to myself, 'you've got to do it tonight.' At two in the morning, I heaved that trunk down. God, it was heavy, but I didn't let that worry me. There I was, with that dead weight on my back, walking briskly, praying all the time. Please, God, no police, not tonight. And God heard me. I crossed the street and was walking past a mosque when I had an inspiration. I put the trunk down, took Girdhari out, I mean all three pieces of him, and chucked them over the low protective wall right inside the mosque.

Truly God is great and moves in strange ways. Next morning I heard that the Hindus had burnt the mosque down. 'There goes poor Girdhari,' I said to myself, 'cremated like a good Hindu.' I advised Rukma to spread word that Girdhari had gone on a trip and hadn't come back as he should have. 'And, sweetheart, I'll be with you nights doing what I like best,' I added. 'Not so soon,' Rukma said. 'We must not see each other for at least fifteen days.'

Seventeen days passed and nothing happened. I had nightmares about Girdhari but I told him, 'You are dead Girdhari, so don't try to scare me. There is nothing you can do to me because you are no longer around. Ha, ha!'

A day later, I was sleeping in my usual place when Rukma woke me up around midnight. She asked me to follow her to her room. Then she lay down on that mattress of hers, naked as on the day she was born. 'I ache all over, darling, rub some oil on my body to soothe the pain,' she whispered in a husky voice. Quite happily I began to massage her all over. In an hour I was exhausted, with sweat dripping out of every pore in my body on to hers, but she did not say, 'That was nice, Abdul Karim, but you must be worn out. That's enough.'

'I am done for, Rukma darling,' I finally said. She gave me one of those smiles. Then she pulled me down next to her and before I knew it I was sound asleep, one of my hands on her breasts.

I woke up with a start because there was something sharp and metallic around my throat but before I could do anything, Rukma had jumped on my chest and was tightening the noose. That was how she had killed Girdhari. I couldn't scream, though I tried to. Then everything went black.

When I came to, it was about four in the morning and I ached all over. Suddenly, there were voices. I lay without daring to breathe, so scared was I. I couldn't see anything but then I realized what was going on only a few feet from me. A man and a woman, locked in each other's arms, breathing heavily and making love. I heard Rukma's voice. 'Tuka Ram, switch on the light.' And his frightened voice, 'No, no, Rukma, please!' 'You big coward!' Rukma replied angrily. 'How are you going to chop him up in three pieces and carry him out for disposal?'

I must have fainted briefly, for the next thing I remember is the light coming in. That made me sit up. Tuka Ram shrieked with fright and ran out of the room. Rukma bolted the door calmly. This Tuka Ram character I knew. He was a mango seller, the kind who went from house to house.

Rukma was looking at me as if she did not believe her eyes. She was sure she had killed me but there I was, sitting bolt upright. I didn't know what she was going to do to me because there was a knock at the door and I heard several voices. Rukma pushed me into the bathroom, telling me to stay there.

It was the neighbours wanting to know if everything was all right because they had heard strange noises. 'I must have been walking in my sleep,' she told them and they left. Then she bolted the door. I was very frightened. I knew she was going to kill me, but strangely, this conviction brought back my physical strength. I stepped out of the bathroom. She didn't hear me. She was leaning out of the window. I rushed forward, put my hands on her buttocks and, with all my strength, heaved her up and pushed her out. There was a loud thud and that was that. I stalked out of her room unobserved.

I lay low for the better part of the morning. My throat was marked because the wire had cut into it. I put a handkerchief around it after massaging it with oil. I was sure that when Rukma was discovered in the morning everyone would think she had fallen out of the window because had she not told the neighbours she walked in her sleep? By midday nothing had happened. Had they found Rukma? She must have fallen into the dead-end street at the back of two buildings, mostly used as a huge refuse bin by the residents, but it was swept every morning. So why hadn't they found Rukma? Maybe it hadn't been cleaned today.

Even by the afternoon nothing had happened. There was only one thing to do. Check out that back street myself. I steeled myself for the shock of discovering her broken body lying on flat stone but there was nothing, no sign of her at all. What could have happened? I swear on the Holy Book if I escape from this mess I have got myself into, Inspector sahib, I'll not be half as surprised as I am about the disappearance of that woman's body. After all, she fell from the third floor and it is logical that the impact should have killed her. That being so, why didn't I find her? Perhaps she is alive, the witch. The neighbours think she has either been abducted by a Muslim or been killed in the riots. If she is dead, well that is the best that could have happened, and if she has been abducted, then God help the man who took her. I know what lies in store for him.

Yes, sir, I must tell you about Tuka Ram. About three weeks after that night I ran into him in the street. 'Where is she?' he demanded. 'I don't know where she is,' I replied. 'You know bloody well where she is,' he snarled. 'I swear by the Holy Book I do not know,' I said sincerely but he didn't seem to believe me. 'You liar! You killed her! I am going to the police! You first killed Girdhari, then you killed her!' he hissed.

After he left, I reviewed my situation. There were no two ways about it. I had to kill him. So, Inspector sahib, what was I to do? I put my knife into my pocket and went out looking for Tuka Ram. I finally found him in the evening at, of all places, the public urinal. He was about to answer the call of nature when I got him. 'Tuka Ram,' I said, 'this is curtains for you.' And I plunged my knife into him. He put both hands on his stomach and fell forward. What a fool I am, Inspector sahib! I should have run but what did I do? I waited around, the knife still in my hand. I even bent down to feel his pulse, just to be sure he was dead. And you know, I have no idea where the pulse is—somewhere about the wrist but where exactly, well, I wasn't quite sure.

And just then, as I was fooling around with his wrist, in walks this burly policeman, looking rather keen to do something that nobody else could do for him and he sees me, knife in hand and the rest of it, and I am nabbed, what else!

Read out the Kalima, the word of God, in a loud voice. There is no God but Allah and Mohammed is His Prophet . . . and what I have told you was the truth, nothing but the truth.

A TALE OF 1947

Mumtaz was speaking with great passion, 'Don't tell me a hundred thousand Hindus and the same number of Muslims have been massacred. The great tragedy is not that two hundred thousand people have been killed, but that this enormous loss of life has been futile. The Muslims who killed a hundred thousand Hindus must have believed that they had exterminated the Hindu religion. But the Hindu religion is alive and well and will remain alive and well. And after putting away a hundred thousand Muslims, the Hindus must have celebrated the liquidation of Islam; but the fact is that Islam has not been affected in the least. Only the naive can believe that religion can be eliminated with a gun. Why can't they understand that faith, belief, devotion, call it what you will, is a thing of the spirit; it is not physical. Guns and knives are powerless to destroy it.'

Mumtaz was very emotional that day. The three of us had come to see him off. He was sailing for Pakistan, a country we knew nothing about. All three of us were Hindus. We had relatives in West Punjab, now Pakistan; some of them had lost their lives in anti-Hindu riots. Was this why Mumtaz was leaving us?

One day Jugal had received a letter, which said that his uncle who lived in Lahore had been killed. He just couldn't believe it. He had said to Mumtaz, 'If Hindu–Muslim killings start here, I don't know what I'll do.'

'What'll you do?' Mumtaz had asked.

'I don't know. Maybe I'll kill you,' he had replied darkly.

Mumtaz had kept quiet and for the next eight days he hadn't spoken to anyone; on the ninth day he had said he was sailing for Karachi that afternoon.

We had said nothing to him nor spoken about it. Jugal was

intensely conscious of the fact that Mumtaz was leaving because of what he had said: 'Maybe I'll kill you.' He wasn't even sure if the heat of religious frenzy could actually bring him to kill Mumtaz, his best friend. That afternoon Jugal was very quiet; it was only Mumtaz who didn't seem to want to stop talking, especially as the hour of departure drew close.

Mumtaz had started drinking almost from the moment he climbed out of bed. He was packing his things as if it was a picnic he was going on, telling jokes, then laughing at them himself. Had a stranger seen him that morning, he would have concluded that his departure from Bombay was the best thing that had ever happened to him. However, none of us was fooled by his boisterousness; we knew he was trying to hide his feelings, even deceive himself.

I tried a couple of times to talk about his sudden decision to leave Bombay but he didn't give me an opportunity.

Jugal fell into an even deeper silence after three or four drinks and in fact left us to lie down in the next room. Brij Mohan and I stayed with Mumtaz. There was much to do. Mumtaz wanted to pay his doctor's bill; his clothes were still at the laundry, etc. He went through all these chores with the utmost aplomb. However, when we went to buy cigarettes from our regular shop on the corner, he put his hand on Brij Mohan's shoulder and said, 'Do you remember, Brij . . . ten years ago when we were all starving, this shopkeeper, Gobind, lent us money?' His eyes were moist.

He didn't speak again till we got home—and then it was another marathon, an unending monologue on everything under the sun. Not much of what he was saying made a great deal of sense, but he was talking with such utter sincerity that both Brij Mohan and I had no option but to let him go on, getting in a word edgeways when we could. When it was time to leave, Jugal came in, but as we got into the taxi to go to the port everyone became very quiet.

Mumtaz was looking out of the window, silently saying goodbye to Bombay, its wide avenues, its magnificent buildings. The port was crowded with refugees, mostly poor, trying to leave for Pakistan. But as far as I was concerned, only one man was leaving today, going to a country where no matter how long he lived he would always be a stranger.

After his baggage was checked in, Mumtaz asked us to come to the deck. Taking Jugal's hand, he said, 'Can you see where the sea and the sky meet? It is only an illusion because they can't really meet but isn't it beautiful, this union which isn't really there?'

Jugal kept quiet. Perhaps he was thinking, 'If it came to that, I may really kill you.'

Mumtaz ordered cognac from the bar because that was what he had been drinking since morning. We stood there, all four of us, glasses in our hands. The refugees had started to board. Jugal suddenly drank his glass down and said to Mumtaz, 'Forgive me. I think I hurt you very deeply that day.'

After a long pause, Mumtaz asked, 'That day when you said, "Maybe I'll kill you," did you really mean that? I want to know.'

Jugal nodded. 'Yes, I am sorry.'

'If you had killed me, you would have been even sorrier,' Mumtaz said philosophically. 'You would have realized that it wasn't Mumtaz, a Muslim, a friend of yours, but a human being you had killed. I mean, if he was a bastard, by killing him you wouldn't have killed the bastard in him; similarly, assuming that he was a Muslim, you wouldn't have killed his Muslimness, but him. If his dead body had fallen into the hands of Muslims, another grave would have sprung up in the graveyard, but the world would have been diminished by one human being.'

He paused for breath, then continued, 'It is possible that after you had killed me, my fellow Muslims may have called me a martyr. But had that happened, I swear to God, I would have leapt out of my grave and begun to scream, "I do not want this degree you are conferring on me because I never even took the examination." In Lahore, a Muslim murdered your uncle. You heard the news in Bombay and killed me. Tell me, what medals would that have entitled you to? And what about your uncle and his killer in Lahore? What honour would be conferred on them? I would say that those who died were killed like dogs and those who killed killed in vain.'

'You are right,' I said.

'No, not at all,' he said in a tense voice. 'I am probably right but what I really wanted to say, I have not expressed very well. When I say religion or faith I do not mean this infection, which afflicts ninety-nine per cent of us. To me, faith is what makes a human being special, distinguishes him from the herd, proves his humanity.'

Then a strange light came into his eyes. 'Let me tell you about this man. He was a diehard Hindu of the most disreputable profession, but he had a resplendent soul.'

'Who are you talking about?' I asked.

'A pimp,' Mumtaz said.

We were startled. 'Did you say a pimp?' I asked.

He nodded. 'Yes, but what a man, though to the world he was a pimp, a procurer of women!' Then Mumtaz began his story.

'I don't remember his full name. It was something Sehai. He came from Madras and was a man of extremely fastidious habits. Although his flat was very small, everything was in its right place, neatly arranged. There were no beds, but lots of floor cushions, all spotlessly clean. A servant was around but Sehai did most things himself, especially cleaning and dusting. He was very straight, never cheated and never told you anything that was not entirely true. For instance, if it was very late and the liquor had run out, he would say, "Sahib, don't waste your money because in this neighbourhood they will only sell you rubbish at this hour." If he had any doubts about a particular girl, he would tell you about her. He told me once that he had already saved up twenty thousand rupees. It had taken him three years, operating at twenty-five per cent. "I need to make only another ten thousand and then I'll go to Benaras and start my own retail cloth business." Why he wanted to earn no more than that I didn't know nor did I have any idea what he found so attractive about the retail cloth trade.'

'A strange man,' I said.

Mumtaz continued, 'First I thought he cannot really be what he appears to be. Maybe he is nothing but a big fraud. After all, it was hard to believe that he considered and treated all the girls that he supplied to his customers as his own daughters. I also found it strange that he had opened a postal savings account for each of them and insisted that they should put their earnings there. There were some whose personal expenses he subsidized. All this was unreal to me because in the real world these things do not happen. One day when I went to see him, he said to me, "Both Ameena and Sakeena have their weekly day off. You see, being Muslims, they like to eat meat once in a while but none is cooked in this house because the rest of us are all strictly vegetarian." One day he told me that the Hindu girl from Ahmedabad, whose marriage he had arranged with a Muslim client of his, had written from Lahore, "I went to the shrine of the great saint Data Sahib and made a wish, which has come true. I am going again to make another wish, which is that you should quickly make thirty thousand so that you can go to Benaras and start that retail cloth business of yours." I had laughed, thinking that he was only telling me this story about the popular Muslim saint because I was a Muslim.'

'Were you wrong?' I asked Mumtaz.

'Yes—he really was what he appeared to be. I am sure he had his faults but he was a wonderful man.'

'How did you find out that he wasn't a fraud?' Jugal, who hadn't spoken until now, asked.

'Through his death,' Mumtaz replied. 'The Hindu–Muslim killings had started. Early one morning, I was hurriedly walking through Bhindi Bazaar, which was still deserted because of the night curfew. There were no trams running and taxis were out of the question. In front of the J.J. Hospital I saw a man lying in a heap on the footpath. I first thought it was a patiwala, who was still sleeping, but then I saw blood and stopped. I detected a slight movement and bent down to look at the man's face. It was Sehai, I realized with a shock. I sat down on the bare footpath. The starched and spotless twill shirt that he habitually wore was drenched in blood. He was moaning. I shook him gently by the shoulder and called his name a couple of times. At first, there was no response but then he opened his eyes; they were expressionless. Suddenly his whole body shook and I knew he had recognized me, "It's you," he whispered.

'I showered him with questions. What had brought him to this preponderantly Muslim locality at a time when people preferred to stay in their own neighbourhoods? Who had stabbed him? How long had he been lying here? But all he said was, "My day is done; this was Bhagwan's will."

'I did not know what Bhagwan's will was but I knew mine. I was a Muslim. This was a Muslim neighbourhood. I simply could not bear the thought that I, a Muslim, should stand here and watch a man, whom I knew to be a Hindu, lie dying at the hands of an assassin who must have been a Muslim. I, who was watching Sehai die, was a Muslim like his killer. The thought did cross my mind that if the police arrived on the scene I'd be picked up, if not on a murder charge, certainly for questioning. And what if I took him to the hospital? Would he, by way of revenge against Muslims, name me as his killer? He was dying anyway. I had an irresistible urge to run, to save my own skin, and I might have done that except that he called me by my name. With an almost superhuman effort, he unbuttoned his shirt, slipped his hand in but did not have the strength to pull it out. Then he said in a voice so faint I could hardly hear it, "There's a packet in here . . . it contains Sultana's ornaments and her twelve hundred rupees . . . they were with a friend for safe custody . . . I picked them up today and was going to return them to her . . . these are bad times you know . . . I wanted her to have her money and the ornaments . . . would you please give them to her . . . tell her she should leave for a safe place . . . but . . . please . . . look after yourself first!"'

Mumtaz fell silent but I had the strange feeling that his voice had become one with the dying voice of Sehai, lying on the footpath in front of the J.J. Hospital, and together the two voices had travelled to that distant blue point where sea and sky met.

Mumtaz said, 'I took the money and ornaments to Sultana, who was one of Sehai's girls, and she started crying.'

We stepped down the gangplank. Mumtaz was waving.

'Don't you have the feeling he is waving to Sehai?' I asked Jugal.

'I wish I were Sehai,' he said.

THE NEW CONSTITUTION

Mangu the tongawala was considered a man of great wisdom among his friends. He had never seen the inside of a school, and in strictly academic terms was no more than a cipher, but there was nothing under the sun he did not know something about. All his fellow tongawalas at the adda, or tonga stand, were well aware of his versatility in worldly matters. He was always able to satisfy their curiosity about what was going on.

Recently, when he had learnt from one of his fares about a rumour that war was about to break out in Spain, he had patted Gama Chaudhry across his broad shoulders and predicted in a statesmanlike manner, 'You will see, Chaudhry, a war is going to break out in Spain in a few days.' And when Gama Chaudhry had asked him where Spain was, Ustad Mangu had replied very soberly: 'In Vilayat, where else?'

When war finally broke out in Spain and everybody came to know of it, every tonga driver at the Station adda, smoking his hookah, became convinced in his heart of Ustad Mangu's greatness. At that hour, Ustad Mangu was driving his tonga on the dazzling surface of the Mall, exchanging views with his fare about the latest Hindu–Muslim rioting.

That evening when he returned to the adda, his face looked visibly perturbed. He sat down with his friends, took a long drag on the hookah, removed his khaki turban and said in a worried voice, 'It is no doubt the result of a holy man's curse that Hindus and Muslims keep slashing each other up every other day. I have heard it said by my elders that Akbar Badshah once showed disrespect to a saint, who angrily cursed him in these words: "Get out of my sight! And, yes, your Hindustan will always be plagued by riots and disorder." And you can see for yourselves. Ever since the end of Akbar's raj, what else has India known but riot after riot!'

He took a deep breath, drew on his hookah reflectively and said, 'These Congressites want to win India its freedom. Well, you take my word, they will get nowhere even if they keep bashing their heads against the wall for a thousand years. At the most, the Angrez will leave, but then you will get maybe the Italywala or the Russiawala. I have heard that the Russiawala is one tough fellow. But Hindustan will always remain enslaved. Yes, I forgot to tell you that part of the saint's curse on Akbar which said that India will always be ruled by foreigners.'

Ustad Mangu had intense hatred for the British. He used to tell his friends that he hated them because they were ruling Hindustan against the will of the Indians and missed no opportunity to commit atrocities. However, the fact was that it was the gora soldiers of the cantonment who were responsible for Ustad Mangu's rather low opinion of the British. They used to treat him like some lower creation of God, even worse than a dog. Nor was Ustad Mangu overly fond of their fair complexion. He would feel nauseated at the sight of a fair and ruddy gora soldier's face. 'Their red wrinkled faces remind me of a dead body whose skin is rotting away,' he used to say.

After an argument with a drunken gora, he would remain depressed for the entire day. He would return to his adda in the evening and curse the man to his heart's content, while smoking his Marble brand cigarette or taking long drags on his hookah.

He would deliver himself of a heavyweight curse, shake his head with its loosely tied turban and say, 'Look at them, came to the door to borrow a light and the next thing you knew they owned the whole house. I am sick and tired of these offshoots of monkeys. The way they order us around, you would think we were their fathers' servants!'

But even after such outbursts, his anger would show no sign of abating. As long as a friend was keeping him company, he would keep at it. 'Look at this one, resembles a leper! Dead and rotting. I could knock him out cold with one blow, but the way he was throwing his git-pit at me, you would have thought he was going to kill me. I swear on your head, my first urge was to smash the damn fellow's skull, but then I restrained myself. I mean it would have been below my dignity to hit this wretch.' He would wipe his nose with the sleeve of his khaki uniform jacket and keep murmuring curses. 'As God is my witness, I'm sick of suffering and humouring these Lat sahibs. Every time I look at their blighted faces, my blood begins to boil in my veins. We need a new law to get rid of these people. Only that can revive us, I swear on your life.'

One day Ustad Mangu picked up two fares from the district courts. He gathered from their conversation that there was going to be a new constitution for India and he felt overwhelmed with joy at the news. The two Marwaris were in town to pursue a civil suit in the local court and, while on their way home, they were discussing the new constitution, the India Act.

'It is said that from 1 April, there's going to be a new constitution. Will that change everything?'

'Not everything, but they say a lot will change. The Indians will be free.'

'What about interest?' asked one.

'Well, this needs to be found out. Should ask some lawyer tomorrow.'

The conversation between the two Marwaris sent Ustad Mangu to seventh heaven. Normally, he was in the habit of abusing his horse for being slow and was not averse to making liberal use of the whip, but not today. Every now and then, he would look back at his two passengers, caress his moustache and loosen the horse's reins affectionately. 'Come on son, come on, show 'em how you take to the air.'

After dropping his fares, he stopped at his friend Dino the sweetmeat vendor's shop in Anarkali. He ordered a large glass of lassi, drank it down, belched with satisfaction, took the ends of his moustache in his mouth, sucked on them and said in a loud voice, 'The hell with 'em all!'

When he returned to the adda in the evening, contrary to routine, no one that he knew was around. A storm was roaring in his breast and he was dying to share the great news with his friends, that really great news which he simply had to get out of his system. But no one was around to hear it.

For about half an hour, he paced about restlessly under the tin roof of the Station adda, his whip under his arm. His mind was on many things, good things that lay in the future. The news that a new constitution was to be implemented had brought him to the doorstep of a new world. He had switched on all the lights in his brain to carefully study the implications of the new law that was going to become operational in India from 1 April. The worried words of the Marwari about a change in the law governing interest or usury rang in his ears. A wave of happiness was coursing through his entire body. Quite a few times, he laughed under his thick moustache and hurled a few words of abuse at the Marwaris. 'The new constitution is going to be like boiling hot water is to bugs who suck the blood of the poor,' he said to himself.

He was very happy. A delightful cool settled over his heart when he thought of how the new constitution would send these white mice (he always called them by that name) scurrying back into their holes for all times to come.

When the bald-headed Nathoo ambled into the adda some time later, his turban tucked under his arm, Ustad Mangu shook his hand vigorously and said in a loud voice, 'Give me your hand, I have great news for you that will not only bring you immense joy but might even make hair grow back on your bald skull.'

Then, thoroughly enjoying himself, he went into a detailed description of the changes the new constitution was going to bring. 'You just wait and see. Things are going to happen. You have my word, this Russian king is bound to do something big.' And as he talked, he continued to slap Nathoo's bald head, and with some force as well.

Ustad Mangu had heard many stories about the socialist system the Soviets had set up. There were many things he liked about their new laws and many of the new things they were doing, which was what had made him link the king of Russia with the India Act or the new constitution. He was convinced that the changes being brought in on 1 April were a direct result of the influence of the Russian king.

For the past several years, the Red Shirt movement in Peshawar and other cities had been much in the news. To Ustad Mangu, this movement was all tied up with the 'king of Russia' and, naturally, with the new constitution. Then there were the frequent reports of bomb blasts in various Indian cities. Whenever Ustad Mangu heard that so many had been caught somewhere for possessing explosives or so many were going to be tried for treason, he interpreted it all to his great delight as preparation for the new constitution.

One day he had two barristers in the back of his tonga. They were vigorously criticizing the new constitution. He listened to them in silence. One of them was saying, 'It is Section II of the Act that I still can't make sense of. It relates to the federation of India. No such federation exists in the world. From a political angle too, such a federation would be utterly wrong. In fact, one can say that this is going to be no federation.'

Since most of this conversation was being carried on in English, Ustad Mangu had only been able to follow the last bit. He came to the conclusion that these two barristers were opposed to the new constitution and did not want their country to be free. 'Toady wretches,' he muttered with contempt. Whenever he called someone a 'toady wretch' under his breath, he felt greatly elated that he had applied the words correctly and that he could tell a good man from a toady.

Three days after this incident, he picked up three students from Government College who wanted to be taken to Mozang. He listened to them carefully as they talked.

'The new constitution has raised my hopes. If so and so becomes a member of the assembly, I will certainly be able to get a job in a government office.'

'Oh! There are going to be many openings and, in that confusion, we will be able to lay our hands on something.'

'Yes, yes, why not!'

'And there's bound to be a reduction in the number of all those unemployed graduates who have nowhere to go.'

This conversation was most thrilling as far as Ustad Mangu was concerned. The new constitution now appeared to him to be something bright and full of promise. The only thing he could compare the new constitution with was the splendid brass and gilt fittings he had purchased after careful examination a couple of years ago for his tonga from Choudhry Khuda Bux. When the fittings were new, the nickel-headed nails would shimmer and where brass had been worked into the fittings it shone like gold. On the basis of that analogy, it was essential that the new constitution should shine and glow.

By 1 April, Ustad Mangu had heard a great deal about the new constitution, both for and against. However, nothing could change the concept of the new constitution that he had formed in his mind. He was confident that come 1 April, everything would become clear. He was sure that what the new constitution would usher in would soothe his heart.

At last, the thirty-one days of March drew to a close. There were still a few silent night hours left before the dawn of 1 April and the weather was unusually cool, the breeze quite fresh. Ustad Mangu rose early, went to the stable, set up his tonga and took to the road. He was extraordinarily happy today because he was going to witness the coming in of the new constitution.

In the cold morning fog, he went round the broad and narrow streets of the city but everything looked old, like the sky. His eyes wanted to see things taking on a new colour but, except for the new plume made of colourful feathers that rested on his horse's head, everything looked old. He had bought this new plume from Chaudhry Khuda Bux for fourteen annas and a half to celebrate the new constitution.

The road lay black under his horse's hooves. The lamp posts that stood on the sides at regular intervals looked the same. The shop signs had not changed. The way people moved about, the sound made by the tiny bells tied around his horse's neck were not new either. Nothing was new, but Ustad Mangu was not disappointed.

Perhaps it was too early in the morning. All the shops were still closed. This he found consoling. It also occurred to him that the courts did not start work until nine, so how could the new constitution be at work just yet.

He was in front of Government College when the tower clock imperiously struck nine. The students walking out through the main entrance were smartly dressed, but somehow their clothes looked shabby to Ustad Mangu. He wanted to see something startling and dramatic.

He turned his tonga left towards Anarkali. Half the shops were already open. There were crowds of people at sweetmeat stalls, and general traders were busy with their customers, their wares displayed invitingly in their windows. Overhead, on the power lines perched several pigeons, quarrelling with each other. But none of this held any interest whatever for Ustad Mangu. He wanted to see the new constitution as clearly as he could see his horse.

Ustad Mangu was one of those people who cannot stand the suspense of waiting. When his first child was to be born he spent the last four or five months in a state of great agitation. While he was sure that the child would come to be born one day, he found it hard to keep waiting. He wanted to take a look at his child, just once. It could then take its time being born. It was because of this desire, which he could not overcome, that he had pressed his sick wife's belly and put his ear to it in an attempt to find out something about the baby, but he had had no luck.

One day he had screamed at his wife in exasperation, 'What's the matter with you! All day long you lie in bed as if you were dead. Why don't you get up and walk about to gain some strength? If you keep lying there like a flat piece of wood, do you think you will be able to give birth?'

Ustad Mangu was temperamentally impatient. He wanted to see every cause have an effect, and he was always curious about it. Once his wife, Gangawati, watching his impatient antics, had said to him, 'You haven't even begun digging the well and already you're dying to have a drink.'

This morning he was not as impatient as he normally would have been. He had come out early to take a look at the new constitution with his own eyes, in the same way he used to wait for hours to catch a glimpse of Gandhiji and Pandit Jawaharlal Nehru being taken out in a procession.

Great leaders, in Ustad Mangu's view, were those who were profusely garlanded when taken out in public. Anyone bedecked in garlands of marigolds was a great man in Ustad Mangu's book. And if because of the milling crowds a couple of near-clashes took place, the leader's stature grew in Ustad Mangu's eyes. He wanted to measure the new constitution by the same yardstick.

From Anarkali he turned towards the Mall, driving his tonga slowly on its shiny surface. In front of an auto showroom, he found a fare bound for the cantonment. They settled the price and were soon on their way. Ustad Mangu whipped his horse into action and said to himself, 'This is just as well. One might find out something about the new constitution in the cantonment.'

He dropped his passenger at his destination, lit a cigarette, which he placed between the last two fingers of his left hand, and eased himself onto a cushion in the rear of the tonga. When Ustad Mangu was not looking for a new fare, or when he wanted to think about some past incident, he would move into the rear seat of the tonga, with the reins of his horse wound around his left hand. On such occasions, his horse, after neighing a little, would begin to move forward at a gentle pace, glad to be spared the daily grind of cantering ahead.

Ustad Mangu was trying to work out if the present system of allotting tonga number plates would change with the new law, when he heard someone calling out to him. When he turned to look, he found a gora standing under a lamp post at the far end of the road, beckoning to him.

As already noted, Ustad Mangu had an intense hatred for the British. When he saw that his new customer was a gora, feelings of hatred rose in his heart. His first instinct was to pay no attention to him and just leave him where he was. But then he felt that it would be foolish to give the man's money a miss. The fourteen annas and a half he had spent on the plume should be recovered from these people, he decided.

He neatly turned around his tonga on the empty road, flicked his whip and was at the lamp post in no time. Without moving from his comfortable perch, he asked in a leisurely manner, 'Sahib Bahadur, where do you want to be taken?'

He had spoken these words with undisguised irony. When he had called him 'Sahib Bahadur', his upper lip, covered by his moustache, had moved lower, while a thin line that ran from his nostril to his lower chin had trembled and deepened, as if someone had run a sharp knife across a brown slab of shisham wood. His entire face was laughing, but inside his chest roared a fire ready to consume the gora.

The gora, who was trying to draw on a cigarette by standing close to the lamp post to protect himself from the breeze, turned and moved towards the tonga. He was about to place his foot on the foothold when his eyes met Ustad Mangu's and it seemed as if two loaded guns had fired at each other and their discharge had met in mid-air and risen towards the sky in a ball of fire.

Ustad Mangu freed his left hand of the reins that he had wrapped around it and glared at the gora standing in front of him, as if he would eat every bit of him alive. The gora, meanwhile, was busy dusting his blue trousers of something that couldn't be seen, or perhaps he was trying to protect this part of his body from Ustad Mangu's assault.

'Do you want to go or are you again going to make trouble?' the gora asked.

'It is the same man,' Ustad Mangu said to himself. He was quite sure it was the same fellow with whom he had clashed the year before. That uncalled for argument had happened because the gora was sozzled. Ustad Mangu had borne the insults hurled at him in silence. He could have smashed the man into little bits, but he had remained passive because he knew that in such quarrels it was tongawalas mostly who suffered the wrath of the law.

'Where do you want to go?' Ustad Mangu asked, thinking about the previous year's argument and the new constitution of 1 April. His tone was sharp like the stroke of a whip.

'Hira Mandi,' the gora answered.

'The fare would be five rupees,' Ustad Mangu's moustache trembled.

'Five rupees! Five rupees! Are you . . .?' the gora screamed in disbelief.

'Yes, yes, five rupees,' Ustad Mangu said, clenching his big right fist tightly. 'Are you interested or will you keep making idle talk?'

The gora, remembering their last encounter, had decided not to be awed by the barrel-chested Ustad Mangu. He felt that the man's skull was again itching for punishment. This encouraging thought made him advance towards the tonga. With his swagger stick, he motioned Ustad Mangu to get down. The polished cane touched Ustad Mangu's thigh two or three times. Ustad Mangu, standing up, looked down at the short-statured gora as if the sheer weight of a single glance would grind him down. Then his fist rose like an arrow leaving a bow and landed heavily on the gora's chin. He pushed the man aside, got down from his tonga and began to hit him all over his body.

The astonished gora made several efforts to save himself from the heavy blows raining down on him, but when he noticed that his assailant was in a rage bordering on madness and flames were shooting forth from his eyes, he began to scream. His screams only made Ustad Mangu work his arms faster. He was thrashing the gora to his heart's content while shouting, 'The same cockiness even on 1 April! Well, sonny boy, it is our Raj now.'

A crowd gathered. Two policemen appeared from somewhere and with great difficulty managed to rescue the Englishman. There stood Ustad Mangu, one policeman to his left and one to his right, his broad chest heaving because he was breathless. Foaming at the mouth, with his smiling eyes he was looking at the astonished crowd and saying in a breathless voice, 'Those days are gone, friends, when they ruled the roost. There is a new constitution now, fellows, a new constitution.'

The poor gora with his disfigured face was looking foolishly, sometimes at Ustad Mangu, other times at the crowd.

Ustad Mangu was taken by police constables to the station. All along the way, and even inside the station, he kept screaming, 'New constitution, new constitution!' but nobody paid any attention to him.

'New constitution, new constitution! What rubbish are you talking? It's the same old constitution.'

And he was locked up.

SWEET MOMENT

XXX . . . XXX . . . Reports are coming in of sweets having been distributed in the Indian cities of Amritsar, Gwalior and Bombay to celebrate the death of Mahatma Gandhi . . . X X X . . . X X X

WAGES

There was looting and rioting everywhere and to them had now been added widespread arson.

Quite unmindful of it all, a man was waltzing down the street, a harmonium strung around his neck, and a popular song on his lips:

She went away to a far land
Breaking my heart
Never again will I love another,
Never again . . .

A young boy went running by, cradling dozens of packets of papads in his arms. He tripped slightly and dropped one packet. As he stooped to try and pick it up, an older man with an obviously stolen sewing machine on his head said, 'Why bother to do that son? The road is so hot that your papads will soon turn to a crisp.'

A gunnybag landed on the street with a thud. A man stepped forward and slashed it open with his big hunting knife, expecting perhaps to find a bleeding fugitive inside, but what came cascading out was sugar: white, fine-grained sugar. Soon a crowd gathered and people began to help themselves to the unexpected prize. One man in the crowd was only wearing a length of cloth loosely wrapped around his middle. As if it was the most normal thing to do, he freed himself of it and, standing stark naked, began to throw fistfuls of sugar into what was now a makeshift carrier-bag.

'Make way, make way, look out, look out.' It was a tonga, loaded with gleaming furniture made of fine wood.

From the top-floor window of a house overlooking the street, someone threw down a rolled length of muslin, but on its way down it was licked by flames leaping out of a lower-storey window, and by the time it hit the ground it was nothing but a handful of ash.

They finally managed to haul the big steel safe out of the house and although there were many of them, all armed with sticks, they just could not get it to open.

One man stepped out of a shop carrying several tins of Cow & Gate dry milk. No one paid any attention to him as he disappeared down the street, taking slow, careful steps.

'Come on, boys, treat yourself to cool lemonade. It is summer time,' came the loud invitation. One man with a car tyre around his neck picked up two bottles and walked off without even saying thank you.

Someone screamed, 'Send for the fire brigade; otherwise all these precious goods will be lost to the flames.' However, no attention whatsoever was paid to this eminently sensible suggestion.

And so it went on all day with the heat from the sun and the many fires blazing in all directions becoming almost unbearable. Suddenly, there was the sound of gunfire. By the time the police appeared, the street was quite deserted . . . except for a receding human figure at the other end moving very fast. The policemen, furiously blowing their whistles, ran towards what looked like an apparition appearing and disappearing through the haze and the smoke. And then he was in the clear, a Kashmiri seasonal labourer, one of thousands who came to the plains in search of daily work. There was a big gunnybag on his back. The policemen began to blow their whistles even more furiously but he did not stop. He was running as if what he was carrying on his back was no heavier than a feather.

The policemen began to tire. Even their whistles seemed to have gone hoarse. In exasperation, one of them pulled out his revolver and fired, hitting the Kashmiri labourer in the leg. The gunnybag fell off his back. He stopped, saw blood gushing out of the wound, but paid no attention to it. Picking up the gunnybag with one mighty heave, he broke into a sprint.

'Let him go to hell,' the policemen said, but just then he staggered and fell to the ground in a heap, with the gunnybag resting on top of him.

The policemen took both the man and the gunnybag to the station. On the way, several times, he tried to soften the hearts of his captors but to no avail. 'Exalted sirs, why you catch this poor fellow? All he take is one little bag of rice. Brave ones, why you shoot down this poor man when all he done . . .'

At the station, he made many efforts to present his case. 'Exalted sirs, other people steal big things. All poor me take is one bag of rice. Me very poor man, just eat rice . . .'

Ultimately, he gave up. Wiping his brow with his dirty skullcap, he looked at the bag of rice longingly and, spreading both his hands in supplication before the police inspector, said, 'All right, exalted sir, you keep the rice, all poor me ask is my wages for carrying this bag . . . just four annas.'

COOPERATION

A crowd, forty or fifty strong, armed with sticks, advanced determinedly towards the big residential house. Its intention was quite obvious: looting.

Suddenly, a slim, middle-aged man emerged from the midst of the throng, pushed everyone aside, waved his arms high over his head as politicians do and began to speak. 'Brothers,' he said, very much in the style of a populist leader, 'there is great wealth in this house, much that is precious. Let's take it all and then divide it equally among ourselves.'

Sticks waved in the air, clenched fists bobbed up and down and loud slogans greeted the suggestion.

The crowd led by the slim, middle-aged man began to close in on the house, which was said to contain immense wealth.

As they came to the front door, the slim man spoke again. 'Brothers, whatever is in there belongs to you; that being so, there is no need to be impatient, no need to get into fights over who should take what. Let's go!'

'But there is a lock on that door,' someone shouted.

'Pull down the door, yes pull it down,' several of the men screamed.

Sticks waved in the air, clenched fists bobbed up and down and loud slogans greeted the suggestion.

The slim man, a faint smile playing on his lips, gestured to the rioters to stay calm. 'Brothers, I am going to unlock this door with the help of a key.'

Then, from his pocket, he produced a bunch of keys, carefully selected one and slipped it into the lock, which gave way. As the heavy wooden door swung back on its hinges, the crowd went mad with excitement.

The slim man wiped his brow with his sleeve and said,

'Brothers, go easy. As everything in there belongs to you, is there any point in getting agitated?'

This had an immediate calming effect on the rioters, who could be seen entering through the main door in an orderly fashion, almost queuing. However, once they were all inside, they turned unruly, ruthless and greedy.

In a voice full of pain, the slim man spoke again. 'Brothers, we should be gentle. There is absolutely no need to fight one another or snatch what the next one is holding. Let's work in a spirit of cooperation. If you see one of you with an object of value, don't envy him. This is a large house, and surely all of you can find something equally valuable. But let's not act like savages; otherwise you will only end up breaking what belongs to you. It will be your loss.'

Discipline returned to the crowd once again. The house began to be emptied of its contents slowly and methodically.

Occasionally, the slim man would offer advice.

'Look, my friend, lift that radio gently or you might damage it. Yes, don't leave the antenna behind.'

'This is a walnut table with ivory inlay work. It folds nicely . . . like this.'

'No, no, don't drink here; it may go to your head. Take the bottle with you.'

'Watch out, let me switch the mains off or you could get a bad shock.'

There was a scuffle in one room, with four of the looters quarrelling over a rolled length of silk. This time there was almost admonition in the slim man's voice. 'You will only end up tearing it to shreds. I am sure there is a tape measure in this house somewhere and a pair of scissors. Let's look for them, measure the cloth and then cut it into four equal parts.'

Suddenly, there was the sound of a dog barking and then like a flash of lightning a big Alsatian leapt into the room. He pounced on three or four of the intruders, pinning them to the floor.

'Tiger, Tiger!' the slim man screamed.

Tiger, who was about to go for the windpipe of one of the terrified men, immediately let go of him and, tail between his legs, eyes to the floor, went to the slim man.

Everyone had run away, except the man whom Tiger had been about to savage.

The solitary intruder looked at the slim man. 'Who are you?'

'I own this house.' He smiled. 'But watch out or you will drop that crystal vase. It seems to be slipping out of your fingers.'

DIVISION

He chose the largest of the wooden chests for himself, but no matter how hard he tried, he couldn't move it.

Another man, who had been unable to find anything worthwhile to take, came up to him. 'Do you need help?'

He said yes and the volunteer picked up the deadweight with his strong hands and with one mighty heave placed it on his broad back.

However, the weight was so crippling that the volunteer felt, as they took to the street, that his back would break or his legs would give way. What kept him going was the expectation of reward.

The man who had spotted the chest was not in very good physical shape; however, in order to assert his ownership, he kept one hand firmly on the prize as they slowly moved towards a safe spot.

Once they were there and the chest had been safely placed on the ground, the man who had done all the hard work said, 'I want to know what my share is.'

'One-fourth,' came the reply.

'That's not enough!'

'No? But remember it was I who found it.'

'Yes, but it was I who brought it all the way here on my back.'

'What about fifty-fifty?'

'That's a deal. Let's see what is inside.'

What came out was a man with a sword, with which he immediately subdivided the two shareholders into four.

PROPER USE

After firing ten rounds and killing three men, the Pathan felt that he too had joined the band of the brave.

There was utter pandemonium. People were running helter-skelter. Some were engaged in looting, some in killing. The Pathan, his gun held proudly in one hand, joined the fray and after wrestling about for an hour or so, managed to win a prize—a thermos flask.

When the police arrived, everyone ran, including the Pathan.

He narrowly escaped being shot through the head, but he did not let go of the red flask.

With much pride, he showed his friends the great prize, at which one among them smiled. 'Khan sahib, what have you got there?'

With loving eyes, the Pathan looked at the shimmering lid of the flask. 'Why?' he asked.

'Don't you know what this is? A special bottle that keeps cold things cold and warm things warm.'

Tucking the flask in his big pocket, the Pathan said, 'Good, it will do nicely. Keep my snuff cold in winter, warm in summer.'

THE BENEFITS OF IGNORANCE

The trigger was pressed and the bullet spun out ill-tempered.

The man leaning through the window doubled over without making a sound.

The trigger was pressed a second time. The bullet swished through the air, puncturing the water-carrier's goatskin. He fell on his face and his blood, mixing with the water, began to flow across the road.

The trigger was pressed a third time. The bullet missed, embedding itself into a mud wall.

The fourth felled an old woman. She did not even scream.

The fifth and sixth were wasted. Nobody got killed and nobody got wounded.

The marksman looked frustrated, when suddenly a running child appeared on the road. He raised his gun and took aim.

'What are you doing?' his companion asked.

'Why?'

'You are out of bullets.'

'You keep quiet. How does a little child know?'

FOR NECESSARY ACTION

When the attack came, some members of the minority community in the neighbourhood were killed, while the survivors ran off. One man and his wife, however, hid themselves in the basement of their house.

For two nights they were cooped up there, expecting to be discovered any moment.

Two more nights went by and the fear of death began to recede, replaced by pangs of hunger.

Four more nights passed, but by now they had reached a point where they did not really care whether they lived or died. They came out of their hideout.

In a voice that could barely be heard, the man said to the new occupants of his house, 'We give ourselves up. Please kill us.'

'Our religion forbids us to kill,' they answered.

They were Jains, but after mutual consultations, the fugitive couple was handed over to residents of a neighbouring locality 'for necessary action'.

MIRACLE MAN

Homes were being raided by the police to recover looted goods.

Out of fear, people started to chuck their 'hot cargo' out of their windows after nightfall. There were some whose keenness to stay out of the law's mischief was so great that they even got rid of legitimately acquired goods.

One man, however, had a problem. He had two large sacks of sugar in his house, which he had helped himself to when the local grocery store was ransacked. One night, he managed to drag them to the neighbourhood well. One he pushed down the shaft quite easily, but fell in himself with the second.

His screams woke up everyone. Ropes were lowered but to no avail. Finally, two youths went down and pulled him out, but he died a few hours later.

The next morning when people drew out their drinking water from the well, it was found to be sweet.

That night, there were prayer lamps illuminating the miracle man's grave.

MISTAKE REMOVED

'Who are you?'

'And who are you?'

'Har Har Mahadev, Har Har Mahadev!'

'Har Har Mahadev!'

'What is the evidence that you are who you say you are?'

'Evidence? My name is Dharam Chand.'

'That is no evidence.'

'All right, I know all the four Vedas by heart, test me out.'

'We know nothing about the Vedas. We want evidence.'

'What?'

'Lower your trousers.'

When his trousers were lowered, there was pandemonium. 'Kill him, kill him.'

'Wait, please wait . . . I am your brother . . . I swear by Bhagwan, I am your brother.'

'Then what is this?'

'The area through which I had to pass was controlled by our enemies; therefore, I had to take this precaution . . . just to save my life . . . this is the only mistake, the rest is in order.'

'Remove the mistake.'

The mistake was removed . . . and with it Dharam Chand.

JELLY

At six in the morning, the man who used to sell ice from a pushcart next to the service station was stabbed to death. His body lay on the road, while water kept falling on it in steady driblets from the melting ice.

At a quarter past seven, the police took him away. The ice and blood stayed on the road.

A mother and child rode past the spot in a tonga. The child noticed the coagulated blood on the road, tugged at his mother's sleeve and said, 'Look, mummy, jelly.'

INVITATION TO ACTION

When the neighbourhood was set on fire, everything burned down with the exception of one shop and its sign.

It said: 'All building and construction materials sold here'.

'Hey, you there, speak at once, who're you?'

'I . . . I . . .'

'You offshoot of the devil, at once . . . are you Indoo or Musalmeen?'

'Musalmeen.'

'Who is your Prophet?'

'Mohammad Khan.'

'OK, let him go.'

WARNING

After a great deal of struggle, the owner of the house was dragged out and kicked to the ground.

But he got up immediately, dusted off his clothes with great dignity and wagging a finger at the rioters said, 'You can kill me, but I am warning you, don't you dare touch my money!'

PERMANENT VACATION

'Catch him, catch him, don't let him get away!'

After a brief chase, the quarry was overtaken and was about to be lanced to death when he said in a tremulous voice, 'Please don't kill me, don't kill me please . . . you see I am going home on vacation.'

RITUALISTIC DIFFERENCE

'I placed my knife across his windpipe and, slowly, very slowly, I slaughtered him.'

'And why did you do that?'

'What do you mean why?'

'Why did you kill him the halal way?'

'Because I enjoy doing it that way.'

'You idiot, you should have chopped his neck off with one single blow. Like this.'

And the halal killer was dispatched in accordance with the correct ritual.

LOSING PROPOSITION

The two friends finally picked out a girl from the dozen or so they had been shown. She cost forty-two rupees and they brought her to their place.

After spending the night with her, one of them asked her, 'What is your name?'

When she told him, he was taken aback. 'But we were told you were the other religion.'

'They lied,' she replied.

'The bastards cheated us!' he screamed as he ran to his friend, 'selling us a girl from our own faith. Let's go and return her!'

BESTIALITY

With great difficulty, the husband and wife managed to get away with a few household valuables. The teenage daughter was nowhere to be found. The baby girl, however, the mother kept close to her breast. The brown buffalo they had was taken away by the rioters. The cow was still with them, but her calf had gone missing.

All four—the husband, the wife, the baby girl and the cow—were now in safe hiding. It was very dark. When the little girl began to cry because she was afraid, it was like bongo drums in the night's stillness. The terrified mother covered the baby's mouth with her hand, and for additional protection, the father threw a thick sheet over her.

A few minutes passed. Suddenly, a calf mooed in the near distance. The cow heard him, jumped up, answered the call loudly and began to run around in circles as if she were demented. They tried hard to calm her down but in vain.

The noise alerted their pursuers. In the distance, they could see the glow of hand-held torches.

'Why did you drag this beast along?' the woman asked her husband angrily.

THE FOOL

Commenting on his suicide, a friend of his said, 'What a fool! I kept arguing with him that if his beard had been shaved off and his long hair scissored, it did not mean he had lost his religion. Daily use of yogurt and the benediction of the Guru would return him to the shape he was in.'

MODESTY

The rioters brought the train to a stop. Those who belonged to the other religion were methodically picked out and slaughtered. After it was all over, those who remained were treated to a feast of milk, custard pies and fresh fruit.

Before the train moved off, the leader of the hosts addressed the passengers: 'Brothers and sisters, since we were informed late of your train's arrival time, we were not able to offer you the kind of hospitality we would have wished.'

DETERMINATION

'Under no circumstances am I prepared to be converted to a Sikh. I want my razor back.'

DUE SUPERVISION

Introducing his friend as one belonging to the same religion, A was able to get B a ride with a convoy, which was being moved to safety under military escort.

During the trip, B, whose religion had been changed for the sake of safety, asked the soldiers, 'Have any incidents taken place in this area of late?'

'Nothing much,' the soldiers answered, 'except that a mongrel was gunned down in a nearby neighbourhood the other day.'

Terrified, B asked, 'Anything else?'

'No, only three dead bitches were found floating in the canal.'

'Doesn't the military do anything about it?' A asked the soldiers, hoping to reassure B.

'But of course, everything is done under its due supervision.'

THE GARLAND

The rampaging mob suddenly changed direction, its wrath now directed at the statue of Sir Ganga Ram. Sticks were swung through the air; bricks and stones were put to liberal use. One man smeared the statue's face with coal tar. Another strung together a garland of shoes and was about to place it around the statue's neck when the police arrived, guns blazing.

The man with the garland of shoes was shot, then taken to be bandaged at Sir Ganga Ram Hospital.

OUT OF CONSIDERATION

'Don't kill my daughter in front of my eyes.'

'All right, all right. Peel off her clothes and shoo her aside!'

PRECAUTIONARY ARRANGEMENT

The first incident took place in front of the hotel on the corner. A sentry was immediately put on duty there.

The second incident happened the next evening, not too far from the general store. The sentry was moved to the site of the new occurrence.

The third incident took place at midnight in front of the laundry.

The sentry was ordered to stand guard at the new spot. 'Please post me where the next incident is going to take place,' he suggested.

MISHTAKE

Ripping the belly cleanly, the knife moved in a straight line down the midriff, in the process slashing the cord that held the man's pyjamas in place.

The one with the knife took one look and exclaimed regretfully, 'Tut tut tut! . . . Mishtake.'

TIDINESS

The train was stationary.

Three gunmen appeared on the platform. 'Any turkey in there?' they asked the passengers.

'None,' they replied. One passenger was about to say something but then changed his mind.

A few minutes passed. Suddenly four men holding lances stuck their heads through the windows of the carriage. 'Any turkey in there?' they asked.

The man who had decided to keep quiet the last time spoke now. 'I don't know. Perhaps you could check out the lavatory.'

The men stepped in, broke down the lavatory door and came out with a 'turkey'.

'Slash his throat,' suggested one of the men holding the lances.

'No, no, not here!' said his friend. 'It'll mess up the carriage. Take him out.'

GOD IS GREAT

The evening finally came to an end and the singing girl's clients left one by one.

The old man in charge of the arrangements said, 'We came here after having lost everything on the other side, but Allah has showered us with all these riches in a few days.'

SOCIALISM

He loaded all his belongings on to a truck and was driving to another town when he was waylaid by a mob. Eyeing the goods greedily, one man said to the other, 'Just look at all that booty he is decamping with.'

The owner smiled proudly. 'What you see there is my personal property.'

Two or three men laughed. 'We know it all.'

One man yelled, 'Don't let this rich man get away. He is a robber with a truck.'

DOUBLE CROSS

'Look, this is hardly fair. You sold me impure petrol at black-market price and not even one shop could be put to the torch.'

RESTING TIME

'He is not dead. There is still some life left in him.'

'O leave it, my friend, I am exhausted.'

LUCK

'That is rotten luck, my friend. After so much hard work, all I was able to get was this box . . . and all it contained was pork.'